This is a work of fiction. All of the characters,

organizations, and events portrayed in this novel are

either products of the author's imagination or are used

fictitiously. Any resemblance to actual persons, living or

dead is purely coincidental.

Acknowledgements

I would like to thank God for this incredible vision to write. You showed me that I can do all things through Christ that strengthens me. My creativeness, words and vivid imagination all came from you and I thank you for that. I never thought that I would write a book but you gave me that push and opened doors for me out of nowhere. You are in awesome God.

To My parents: Thank you for your love and support through this journey. You gave me your blessing and encouragement to pursue my dream and I am forever thankful for that. I'm not done yet and there's more to come. To Tameka Jones and Markita Hall: A big shout out goes to you thank y'all so much for believing enough in my writing to tell others to give me a chance and listen to my story. I love y'all. I was just a reader looking for a way to interact with authors and look at me now. I made it!

To my Cinematic Inc. Family: Janisha and Lou, David Weaver, Thank you for giving me a chance to show the world my writing skills. Thanks for putting up with my attitude lol. I appreciate y'all so much.

To the rest of the team: Thanks for your kind words and wisdom. Y'all are always there for me.

A special thanks to my loves: Andrea Wheatley, Michea Lockett, Krystal Burrell, Shelli Marie, Kimberly Jones, Tameka Jones, Platinum, Monica Parker, Chevonne little falls and Erinn McNeal. You have been with me since the beginning. Y'all have listened to me whine, share my crazy ideas, drive myself crazy and pull all-nighters. Y'all never let me give up and pushed me to my full ability. Y'all are like the sisters that I never had and I'm glad I have y'all in my life. If I forgot anyone I apologize a special thanks to all the readers that have been waiting patiently for my release.

Dedication

I dedicate this to everybody that is looking for love. Your Mrs. Right or Mr. Right is coming in due time. This is especially for the physical and mentally disabled people. You can find love. Don't settle for less than what you deserve. You are beautiful on the inside and out.

Prologue:

Six years Earlier…. Real Recognize Real Lies
You wouldn't "Last A Day In My Shoes"

Poem……
The stares, the laughs, the pointing and mocking.
The pain, mental, emotional and physical stress
That's not even half the test.
Your mind is so weak that you can't see past the
physical disability of someone like me.
That's what makes you so ugly
Don't judge me
You don't know what I been through
You wouldn't last a day in my shoes
Be careful what you say to others it could happen to
you.

Glancing in the mirror as she flat ironed her hair,
Lashay began to get ready for her date tonight. She
rocked a pair of dark blue skinny jeans with a long sleeve
white top with matching tall boots with wedge heels. She
was feeling optimistic this time.

"I hope he don't be on no bullshit. I look too cute for my time to be wasted," Lashay said.

Ivan agreed to meet to her at Ruth's Steak house in Troy, Michigan. Just as she looked at the clock, her phone rang. Ivan was calling.

"Hey, I can't wait to see you." Ivan said.

"I know I can't wait to see you either." Lashay said, with a smile in her voice.

"How much longer do I have to wait before I see that beautiful face?" Ivan asked, eagerly.

"As we speak I'm leaving out now." Lashay said into the phone, applying light makeup to her face.

"Okay, see you soon." Ivan said.

"Bye." Lashay replied sweetly, rushing to get done.

Five minutes later, she hopped in her car headed to her destination. It didn't take long for her to get there. When she pulled up to the restaurant, he was standing there waiting with roses. As he opened her car door and gave her a hug, he complimented the way she looked.

Ivan was looking too good for words. His hair was freshly cut, and overall he was well groomed. Standing 6' 1", light skin, long curly hair that was neatly braided, light brown eyes, with a muscular structure. The True Religion cologne lingered in the air as they walked hand in hand inside. Ivan ordered for him and her. Since this was her first time here, she let him recommend her dinner. Sharing an elegant meal, they talked and laughed as they got to know each other more in depth. Ivan was the perfect gentleman all night making sure she was satisfied. They were making plans for the next date when the waiter came to the table with the bill. That's when Ivan excused himself from the table.

"I have to make a phone call real quick, I'll be right back. Take care of this, and I'll meet you outside." Ivan said apologetic, sliding the receipt over to her.

"Hell naw, you got me fucked up! I'm not paying for this shit." Lashay said, shouting looking at him deadly as he walked away.

She couldn't believe she got stuck with this high ass bill.

"Another bad date… I can't win for losing." Lashay said, as she paid the bill and fled from the restaurant.

∎∎∎

Unlocking the door with her key to her friend's apartment, Lashay could hear someone screaming loudly but didn't know who it was. As she walked in, she couldn't believe her eyes at the sight. Her friend, Sharylyn, was getting fucked in the ass by her boyfriend, Reggie. Lashay wished she would have called first before she came. The smell of shit and their sex mixed together was sickening.

Trying so hard not to vomit right there she swallowed hard. Sharylyn or Reggie didn't even know that Lashay was standing there watching them. They were in their own world.

"Ahh yes, keep fucking me just like that." Sharylyn said.

Her ass was tooted up all in the air as her face was buried in the couch.

"You like this don't you with your freaky ass?" Reggie said, pulling her hair as he drilled into her, smacking her on the ass.

"Oh I do daddy, I'm about to cum all over that dick." Sharylyn said.

It was nothing to get all excited over or brag about for her. She was just pretending to enjoy it, she was actually bored. Reggie was about seven and a half inches long. He was good to her for now, and that's the only reason why she stayed honestly.

"Cum for me, baby." He said.

Lashay had enough. That was way too much for her to see and not only that, but she couldn't take that horrible smell a minute longer.

Clearing her throat to get their attention she said, "Ummumm hey, sorry to interrupt."

"Wwwhat you doing here?" Sharylyn asked stuttering.

She was clearly caught off guard from Lashay's presence. She wasn't expecting her. Her boyfriend quickly got up and ran into the bathroom, slamming the door loudly. Nobody said anything, I guess they didn't care who saw them, Lashay thought to herself.

"I need to talk, but if I would have known you were busy, I would have come another day."

She turned her head and looked away as her friend wrapped up her body in a sheet that was on the couch with them.

"I'll tell him to leave for a while."

As she got up to go in the back, Lashay could smell a fishy odor coming off her body. She needed to go wash her ass really good and go to the doctor about that. That smell wasn't right. She hoped she didn't have anything too bad. She was going to tell her about it when she came back in the room. Lashay didn't understand how two people could have sex together when one of them reeked so badly. Maybe it was both of them, who knows, all she knew was they needed to handle that ASAP.

Five minutes later Lashay heard the shower running, she was glad she got the hint. While Sharylyn was in the shower, Lashay grabbed the Lysol disinfectant spray from the kitchen and sprayed it all over the living room. She opened the window to let some fresh air in.

The funk was starting to leave. Shortly after Sharlyn emerged from her room wearing a t-shirt and some shorts, she had her hair done in Seginal Twists, pulled up in a bun on top of her head. They decided to sit on her brown smaller couch that was on the opposite side of the living room. There was no way in hell Lashay was going to sit on the other couch after what she just saw. Lashay began to tell her what happened on her date that she had tonight. It was all bad.

"You ain't gone never find a man. You better take what you can get. Nobody wants to talk to somebody crippled." Sharylyn said laughing.

"Why the fuck would you say some shit like that to me?" Lashay asked, offended and hurt by her words. "You supposed to be my friend. You should be telling me encouraging things. Like, 'you will find somebody one day'. Not putting me down. I know every guy out there not gone like me, and I'm fine with that.
Whoever can't accept my disability, fuck them. It wasn't meant for me to talk to them then…" Lashay said.

"Keep dreaming. A nigga don't want somebody who they got to help all the time. That shit is annoying and too much work. You gone be old and miserable by yoself." Sharyln said, not caring at all.

"Get the fuck out my face with that bullshit. Yo hoe ass, don't know shit about love anyways. You done had to take two trips down to Herman Keifer to get two STD'S treated. Are you still burning?" Lashay asked her.

Sharlyn was speechless feeling ashamed and embarrassed by her actions.

"Let's not forget the three abortions you had in the last year. We only nineteen years old, and yo dumb ass keep letting niggas run up in you raw…" Lashay said, shaking her head.

"At least I know how to fuck and suck dick…" Sharyln said, knowing that was a low blow to Lashay, who was inexperienced when it came to sex.

"Fuck you. You know what, I'm done with you. I see you were never my friend. All you do is talk about me, and I don't need that." Lashay said, with aggression.

"Stop being so sensitive, I was just playing." Sharylyn said, knowing she wasn't.

She did feel bad about what she said, but she couldn't take them back now. That was just how life was.

"Nope, we are so through. Don't call me when you need a ride or when that nigga start beating yo ass again, bitch."

Lashay was so angry she could cry.

"I was using yo' ass anyways, the only reason why I pretended to be your friend in the first place was so I could have a ride to and from work. My man has a car now, so I no longer need you." Sharylyn said, hoping she didn't regret the words that just came out her mouth.

"You need to go get treated for that STD you got; smelling like rotten ass fish." Lashay said yelling. "Let me help you out." Lashay said, running into the bathroom turning on the water and probed the cabinet until she found the Clorox bleach.

The tub started to overflow as she poured half of the bottle inside.

"What the fuck are you doing?" Sharylyn screamed, trying to turn it off swiftly coming in behind her.

"I'm giving you a quick lesson on how to keep a man." Lashay said, as she reached over and shoved her very hard into the water.

"Bitch, I'm gone whoop yo ass." Sharylyn said, struggling to stand up on the slippery surface.

"I like to see you try that one." Lashay said, as she grabbed Sharylyn hair as she hauled off and punched her in the mouth.

"You just jealous because ain't nobody fucking you." Sharylyn said, through a bloody mouth as her lip swelled and bled profusely and tears streamed down her face.

She finally got out the tub.

"We'll see how long that last, you infested hoe." Lashay said, walking to the door. "Mark my words bitch, you will reap what you sewn. I hope nothing bad happen to them two kids you got. If something ever was to happen to you, I sure wouldn't help you." Lashay said.

She couldn't believe her two year friendship was over as she walked to her car.

"I didn't need to be hanging around her crippled ass no way." Sharylyn said to herself.

Sharylyn

Sharylyn jumped up off the couch and slammed the door with anger. She was feeling some type of way, so she decided to call her home-girl Trina to vent.

"Girl, you know this bitch had the nerve to come over here, use her key and interrupt me and my man having a spectacular sex session!" Sharylyn fussed.

"You must be talking about Lashay." Trina laughed.

Sharylyn poured herself a drink and got comfortable so that she could fill her friend in on the whole ordeal. Once she was finished, she felt it was necessary to validate her actions.

"Trina, I know you're probably thinking that was some fucked up shit to say to my friend. Well, let me tell you. Lashay was never my friend in the first place. All I was doing was trying to help her out, and now she's all in her feelings. The chick needs get over it.

I just had to use my options to get what I needed at that time, and that was a ride. A bitch ain't had shit better to do, and she was there so why not take advantage? It ain't my fault her dumb gullible ass fell for the bait. I will admit she looked out for a bitch, but on the real, I ain't never been close to any female, and I never will. It was always get them before they get you. When you ain't never had shit in your life, you get it how you live by any means necessary. You can call me a hoe or whatever you want but shit, at the end of the day I'm still getting paid. While most of y'all half assed backwards, basic bitches out here fucking for free. You should never be broke or hungry as long as you got a pussy. Don't sit and judge me like you ain't never had a STD or an abortion, we all know shit happens. We all done had a black eye or two, but what couple was perfect? None!"

"Wow Sharylyn! That's how you truly feel?" Trina gasped in disbelief.

"Hell yeah! Fuck Lashay with her crippled ass! She can go kick rocks for all I care! She ain't done shit for me lately, so it is what it is!" Sharylyn exclaimed, before disconnecting her call.

Lashay

Lashay had steam coming out of her ears as she sat fuming and writing in her journal. Getting her feelings out seemed to be the only therapeutic thing at the moment. She was definitely on ten.

Fuck that bitch Sharylyn. Don't ever trust a hoe with a crooked smile and a gap between her teeth. Ole fake ass. After all the shit I did for her and her kids... In high school, senior year, I let her crash at my crib when her momma would try to sell her body to the highest bidder for a hit. I helped her out until she got on her feet. I'm good on that ass. Never bite that hand that feeds you. Karma is a bitch, and she's coming in full throttle.

Tainted ass pussy bitch needs to go sit in some bleach water. See people got me fucked up thinking I'm all nice and sweet, but they don't want to see my other side, it ain't nothing pretty. She makes me want to go back and beat her ass, real talk, but I ain't gone do it. She better be lucky I found Jesus today. If I ever see her again I'm gone lay these hands on her. Don't believe me? Just watch. Somebody is gone feel my wrath. I'll tell you one thing; this will be my last day helping somebody. You got one time only to fuck me over and after that it's a wrap. It'll be a cold day in hell before I ever help her again. From now on, I'll be keeping to myself, fuck a friend. I don't need that negative energy around me anyway.

She closed the book with a hard slam as she tucked her thoughts away. Getting into the car, she drove to a secret location to clear her head.

Imperfect

Love has No Limits

By

Shanicia

Chapter 1: Six Years later

Her birth name was Lashay Amour Jones. She was twenty-four years old and resided in downtown Detroit, Michigan. She had a spacious two bedroom loft with an amazing view. It was all hers, she owned it. Lashay worked as a receptionist at Henry Ford Hospital on the main boulevard. She held two certifications, one in Medical Billing and Coding and the other in Medical Assisting.

At that moment, Lashay lived alone, no pets or kids. She pushed a 2005 Honda Accord. Although she realized it was a bit old, it got her where she needed to go. She didn't mind because it alleviated having to depend on anybody or ride the city bus. They are never on time, and they are always overcrowded, loud, and ghetto. Besides, they don't even go to certain areas of the city, and the time slots are limited.

To get ahead in life, Lashay was working on her Associate's degree so she could move up in the company in order to make more money. Outside of her business and schooling, she lived the single life.

Now, you're probably wondering if Lashay was crazy, ugly, fat or gay. She was definitely none of the above. She was a very unique individual despite her disability. The disability that they marked her was called Cerebral Palsy. It was a condition that impaired muscle coordination. Lashay was born with a mild case of cerebral palsy; that mostly affected her lower extremities. Her walk was noticeably different. Lashay dragged her feet when she walked, and she was partially blind in her right eye as well. She was born prematurely at six months, and her body didn't get a chance to develop properly. The end resulted in her being disabled. That never stopped her from being the outgoing, happy and independent person she had become. A lot of things may be a challenge for her, but she always learned a way to figure them out.

There wasn't always going to be someone around to help, so she had taught herself how to be as self-sufficient as possible. She didn't like for people to feel pity for her or play that fake caring role. If you were going to be in her life, then you better come correct. She didn't tolerate games or bullshit from anybody.

She had endured enough in her past and refused to go through it in her present.

Lashay grew up in Ann Arbor, Michigan. Her parents went to Eastern Michigan University, where they met at a party. They were very well off, with several businesses by the time Lashay was born. Lashay wasn't your average girl from the hood that you read about. Her family was considered middle class and lived a very comfortable lifestyle. They instilled responsibility and hard work as she grew up. Things were not handed over to her. She had to earn and work hard for everything she had. Her parents didn't treat her any different because she was disabled. They loved her dearly and didn't regret having her at all. She was taught how to do things like everyone else, just in a different way.

Throughout her childhood, she had physical and speech therapy so that she could improve her skills of walking and talking better and function well, like any other human being. Growing up wasn't easy for Lashay, she dealt with a lot of teasing and bullying from others, but she didn't let that affect the person she was. At times it hurt, but she just pushed through it. Lashay didn't kiss anyone's ass to become her friends.

She didn't have many friends, but the ones she had, she loved.   Lashay didn't want for anything. She just wanted to be independent and do things on her own. She knew if she ever needed anything, she could always go to them. Life didn't give you any handouts. She had to learn how to be a go-getter.

Lashay came in from an eight hour shift, and was very tired. The hospital had been busy all day this Monday. It was after five thirty in the evening when she arrived home. She was happy she stayed in a decent area, and it wasn't too much noise heard all the time. These were the times she wished she had a man to cuddle up with. She was tired of being alone. All she wanted to do was to eat and pass out. As soon as she came in, she kicked off her shoes and clothes. She changed into a pajama set that consisted of a tank top and booty shorts. She put her bonnet on to wrap up her weave. She had just got her sew-in last week and didn't want to mess up her hair. The Hollywood Remy hair wasn't cheap. She had a twelve inch ombre of weave with black at the top and honey blond at the bottom on the tips. She wore it straight in a wrap style.

She was 5'2", Hershey's kissed skin with a pretty face, hazel, almond shaped eyes, and a pretty smile. Full sized breasts, nice thick thighs and ass for days. She wore a size 13/14, thick in all the right places. Her nice curves and her voluptuous body caused her to attract many.

It was the beginning of November and getting cold. The weather changed like a song; it'll be sunny one day, then rain, and snow the next. Lashay was not trying to be sick with a cold; it would have been all bad. She was too tired to get in the shower, so she decided she would take one in the morning. She went in the kitchen and made herself a turkey sandwich. Along with the sandwich, she had some red grapes and bottled water. She was trying to lay off the junk. Chips and juice were her weakness, and she was working on getting better at not eating so much of it. As she was getting comfortable on her queen sized pillow-top bed, her Galaxy S5 cell phone began to ring.

"Ugh, I'm trying to eat. I don't want to be bothered right now." She said aloud and sighed. "Damn who is this?"

Whoever the person was, they were dying to talk to her at that moment. They called her repeatedly three times. The fourth time they called, she decided to call back. It was her friend, Lexi. Lashay rolled her eyes towards the ceiling.

She thought to herself, "I wonder what she about to tell me. Maybe it's about her dead beat baby daddies again."

They had met at a job fair and had been friends ever since. Lexi was twenty years old, tall and a light skinned bombshell. She stood 5 '9, a size eight with double D breasts, flat stomach and a small butt. Lexi rocked a short pixie cut. Her hair was black with dark red highlights. She was a pretty girl with bad taste in men. She had two bad little girls who were too grown and in need of a good ass whopping if you asked her. Anayah was five going on twenty five, and she stayed in grown folks business all day long. Amiya was three going on eighteen. Always dancing like a stripper on a pole, singing the latest song that comes on the radio, and trying to twerk her little butt, but didn't know how to say her alphabet or count to ten.

Lexi lived off section 8 and food stamps. She didn't want to work. All she wanted to do was club her life away.

"Smh, I'm glad I don't have any kids right now." Lashay said to herself.

She wasn't ready for that at that point in her life.

Lashay dialed Lexi number back. It rang three times before she answered.

"Hello," Lexi answered.

"Hey girl, what you doing?" Lashay said, agitated.

"Nothing girl, I just put these kids to sleep. I'm about to call Monty cause I need some money. I'm broke, and I know he got a few dollars to help me out." Lexi said, laying across the couch.

"Okay girl, I'm just chilling I had a long day at work." Lashay said, blocking her out.

She turned on her DVR to watch the recording of a new Love and Hip Hop Atlanta episode she missed. She loved her some ratchet TV. They were all a hot mess but very entertaining.

"I was just seeing what you were up to; I will call you back after I call him." Lexi said, fiddling with her cord to her phone charger.

"Before I get off this phone and forget, thanks for picking up Milian today." Lexi said.

To her relief, that was one less person she didn't have to worry about today.

"You know I don't care for her, I only did it for you." Lashay told her.

She used caution when associating with Milian, that girl was too much for her. Lashay only picked her from the side of the road on the freeway, because she didn't want to leave her high and dry just stranded and something ruthless happened to her. She did have a heart; however, it was only because Lexi had begged her to do it. She could've been inconsiderate about Milian, but she wasn't that type of person. Milian gave Lashay a weird vibe like she was no good.

"Love you sister, you always being the bigger person. I love that." Lexi said.

"Yeah, yeah, ok bye, "Lashay said, not really paying any attention to what Lexi was saying because of the drama that was going on in the show.

"Bye." Lexi said.

Lexi dialed Monty's number from her Samsung. Monty was her second baby daddy. He was tall, 6'1", caramel completion with a low cut fade, sick with waves. He stayed at the gym. He had a body out of this world. He had an eight pack with a muscular athletic build. He was muscular but not too big. He resembled the actor, Columbus Short. (Stomp the Yard). He had a cute face with a good job at Chrysler. He drove a 2014 Range Rover.

Monty's problem was, he was always on some bullshit. One minute he was into her, the next minute he didn't want to be bothered. He played too many games with her feelings, and she didn't have time for that. They met one night at Club Nikki's; it's a popular club downtown that everyone went to on weekends. People could get a variety of music from Hip-hop, R&B, Jazz, to Reggae. It was supposed to be a one night stand that turned into a year of messing around. The sex with her was good, and that's what made him stick around that long. Her head game was lethal, so that didn't hurt either. All that changed when she got pregnant with his baby. A DNA test was done to prove it was his, of course.

29

She became too needy and dependent on him to take care of her and the kids. He was all for taking care of his little princess, Amiya, and at times he would look out for Anayah too.

The reality of the situation was, Anayah wasn't his. After a while, he got tired of playing family man and cut her off. He paid child support and still bought his daughter what she needed and wanted. He got her every other weekend to spend time with her.

Monty liked Lexi, but he knew she wasn't the type to wife. At least, not his wife, he thought. She had potential though, if only she got her shit together. Monty knew Lexi wanted a rich man that would take care of her and her kids for life. She wanted a better life for her kids than what she had growing up. She had a lot of growing up to do, her priorities were all wrong.

In his opinion, Lexi needed to get a job and a reliable car to take better care of her kids and get them where all they needed to go. She needed to be a better role model for her kids, or they will end up like her or worse. He didn't mind helping her at all. He just wanted her to do better.

"Man, I need to leave these hood rats alone."
Monty said aloud, as his phone rang.

He picked it up to see who was calling. An
irritated facial expression displayed as he put the phone
to his ear.

"Hello," Monty said.

"Hey Monty, are you busy right now?" Lexi
asked nervously, feeling the jitters in the pit of her
stomach.

"What's up? Is something wrong with Amiya?"

It was eight O' clock P.M. and they weren't cool
like that to hold a conversation. If it wasn't about his
daughter, he didn't want to talk to Lexi at all, and she
knew it.

"No Monty, nothing is wrong with Miya." Lexi
said, as she got loud and rolled her neck as she talked.

"Why are you calling my line?" Monty asked.

He was getting annoyed as he tapped his fingers
on the kitchen counter.

"Can you give me some money until next week? I
need to pay the DTE bill, I'm short one fifty." Lexi said.
"That was the entire bill for the month." She explained,
feeling embarrassed that she had to ask him for help.

She only had fifty dollars to her name, and she wasn't about to be broke. Lexi had a three bedroom townhouse. She stayed in the Martin Luther King complex downtown.

"Yes, I will help you out this time, for the sake of my daughter." Monty said in a cool tone, but don't get in the habit of asking demeanor.

"Thank you so much!" Lexi said, enthusiastically shouting.

"I will drop it off tomorrow after I get off work." Monty said, with the phone halfway up to his ear.

"Ok, I really appreciate this Monty. See you tomorrow." Lexi said, clicking off the line.

"I need to get my shit together fast. I'm tired of asking and borrowing money from people." Lexi said aloud, as she hung up the phone.

In the morning, bright and early, she was going to go to the Michigan Works building on Fourth Street in the downtown area, to get help with her resume. It was time for her to get a job.

She could do a variety of jobs such as retail, cooking, or secretarial. She could even work at a hospital or nursing home as a CNA. She just got her certification back in August. Lexi was ready for a change and was going to stick with a job this time, she promised herself.

Lexi

Lashay was my bestie. I loved her to death. She inspired me, and I wouldn't trade her for anything. Yeah, I know she got tired of me complaining about my babies daddies and other shit, but every day she motivated me to get my shit together. I'm glad I met her, she's really changing me. She always kept me on my toes, so I wouldn't be acting all ratchet like most of the hood rats around here. I will be going to Michigan Works tomorrow to get this job hunt on board. Something has to change ASAP. This wasn't fair to my kids or myself. I can't keep on depending on somebody to look out for me. If Monty didn't come through, I didn't know what might have happened. He's alright when he wants to be. He's better than my first sorry, no good, trifling baby daddy.

Monty

"Lexi is definitely the last chick I'd ever go raw in again. I don't know what the hell I was thinking when I went in and planted my seeds inside of her. Now I'm stuck with her for the next eighteen years raising our daughter. I hate a needy bitch, and that's what she's turned into. When I first met her, she had a little job, in shit. Then it was like, when I started helping her with the bills, she got comfortable and lazy. At first, it was a few days off here and there, then that turned into not going at all. That's what turned me off and why I don't fuck with her. We might have been able to work on something more if she could have stepped her game up." Monty said to his friend Tez as they grabbed a bite to eat.

"Sound to me like you still want her bro." Tez said, biting into his slice of pizza.

"Naw I'm straight man." Monty said, waving him off.

"Bro, you aint fooling nobody." Tez said, seeing through him.

"Gone with that shit man." Monty said, as he turned in the direction of the TV as it played a highlight of a basketball game.

Chapter 2 Lashay's Love Life

Lashay was sitting at home on the couch in the living room. She was having a glass of Sutter Home Mascoto wine. While reading a book, she thought about the relationships she'd had in her lifetime. In her twenty four years of life, Lashay had never had a true love.

Lashay never had a lot of boyfriends, and it was never anything serious about the relationships. Her first boyfriend, Greg, cheated on her after she gave up her virginity to him at the age of eighteen.

He played football for their east side Detroit high school, Denby. He was 5'8, dark skin with pimples, but he kept his hair cut. He wasn't the cutest, but he was nice to her.

One day after school, she went to surprise him, so they could spend some time together for a little while before she went home. After she caught him fucking her associate, in his bed, at his mother's house, it was a wrap.

Then, her next boyfriend was Rashad, and Lord, he was fine. He was 6 feet tall, light complexioned clear skin, and a slender build. Some would say he was a pretty boy. Rashad was a few years older than Lashay.

He worked for a company called Technicolor and had his own car. Although Rashad was older than Lashay, and had a daughter, that didn't bother her.

The problem occurred when he broke Lashay's heart by telling her he wasn't into her like that, but he liked her for who she was. Lashay was devastated because she was in love with him. Shortly after, they stopped talking because Lashay couldn't deal with it. A few months later, she saw him before he went off to the army, and she never heard from him again.

Lashay moved on and went to Macomb Community College for a while and was doing her school thing. She was doing well in her classes and had a decent social life. She hung out with some friends from time to time but nothing major. She wasn't looking for love at the time, she was just doing her. One day, she was bored and she went on a free dating site called Tagged.

It was just something to do to pass the time. She created her profile and uploaded pictures of herself to put on her page. She always received messages and friend requests, but it wasn't anybody she really wanted to get to know.

One day after work, she decided to log on to see if she had any messages. One particular message caught eye. It was from a guy saying he wanted to get to know her and if it was ok if they talked over the phone. She went to his page to see what he looked like. He was twenty-five, dark skinned, tall, about 6'3" with a fade, and his name was Montrell. The only problem she had with him was that he was a big guy, and he was ugly. He weighed over three hundred pounds. He was always fresh with designer clothes. You would never catch him without a pair of new kicks fresh out the box.

He wasn't her type, but she decided to get to know him anyway. They exchanged numbers and talked on the phone for a couple of weeks before they decided to see each other. He came to visit her on a Friday night, and at the time, she lived with her aunt. Her aunt had got into a car accident and needed help around the house. Lashay agreed to come and stay with her for a while to help out until she got on her feet again. She was only twenty years old at the time. They lived in an apartment complex on Cadieux and Morang area on the east side.

Lashay didn't like him at first, but she thought he was nice. The more time they spent together, the more feelings she developed for him. One day he came to visit her, they were going to see a movie, but before they left, he told her he had something to tell her. Montrell told Lashay that he was a drug dealer. She didn't like the fact that he was, but at the same time she knew everybody had a hustle. That was just how he got his money.

Lashay contemplated on whether she was going to stop talking to him or not. Lashay was not trying to get caught up in the lifestyle of a drug dealers' girlfriend, and she wasn't going to jail for nobody, she didn't care how much she liked him. Even though she was young, she wasn't dumb and far from stupid. Mama didn't raise no fool.

Her gut told her not to get caught up in him, but she didn't listen. They ended up talking for two years straight. In those two years of them talking, she met his family, friends, etc. They hung out and spent a lot of time together. On a Friday evening, Lashay was just lounging around the house when Montrell called.

"Hey Bay." Lashay said, happy he called.

"I want to take you to over my people house with me today. They are having a dinner and game night. I hope you know how to play cards." Montrell said.

"Okay, we can do that. I can play the hell out of some spades, so get ready to get your ass kicked." Lashay said.

"We'll see. I'm on my way to get you, so get ready now, Lashay, you know you take forever to get ready." Montrell said, laughing.

"For your information, big head, I'm already dressed!" Lashay said.

"Alright ma, I'm on my way." Montrell said.

"Okay, I'll be waiting." Lashay said.

"Okay bye," Montrell said.

Shortly after, around five forty five P.M; he picked her up. After about twenty minutes, they arrived at Montell's father's house. She had already met his family a few months prior, so they already knew who she was. People were smoking, drinking, and eating. They played games and just had a great time with one another. His father was sitting in his room on his bed, watching an episode of The First 48, when they walked in.

"Hey Cutie Pie. How are you doing?" Montrell's father asked in a flirty tone.

"Hey Mr. Cole. I'm good and you?" Lashay said.

"I'm good honey." Mr. Cole replied, glancing at the T.V.

"That's good." Lashay replied and looked over at Montrell while wondering if they were going to ever talk to each other.

"What's up son?" Mr. Cole asked Montrell.

"Nothing, pops, just chilling, getting this money out here." Montrell said to his father.

"I feel you, son, I need that money you borrowed the other day. My funds low." Mr. Cole said, talking in code in front of Lashay.

Montrell owed his father ten G's of re-up money, for the twenty kilos of coke his father had purchased through his connect. They did business together, it was nothing personal, and Mr. Cole didn't play about his money, son or not. He was gone get it one way or another. They didn't like discussing their business in front of people, especially women.

"Here is your money, pops. Thanks for the loan." Montrell said, placing the stack of money in his hand.

"Thanks son. " Mr. Cole said.

"No problem pops" Montrell said while looking over at Lashay, who was reading "It Is What It Is." by Ivory B on her IPhone.

She knew they were conducting business. So she minded her own business and paid them no mind. She was so engrossed in her book that she didn't hear Montrell calling her name.

"Lashay, Lashay! " Montrell said, shouting in her ear.

"Trell, stop calling my name like you crazy, you know how I get when I read my books." Lashay said, looking up from her phone.

"I know man, you be blocking a nigga out when he trying to talk to you." Montrell said, caressing her hand in his.

"Boy bye, I give you lots of attention and you know it." Lashay said.

"Whatever you say ma, come on, let's go out there with the rest of the fam." Montrell said.

"Lead the way." Lashay said.

"Go and get some of that delicious food yo auntie cooked. She put her foot in the macaroni and cheese." Mr. Cole said as he rubbed his full belly.

As they walked out, Mr. Cole grabbed Montrell pulled him to the side. Lashay continued walking to interact with the rest of the family.

"Son, you know she's a keeper, don't fuck it up, let them other women go. She got her head on straight. And she going somewhere in life. You don't hear about her in the streets, and she doesn't have any kids. Most importantly, she loves your black ass. If I was younger, I would be all over that." Mr. Cole said, thinking his son was fool for messing things up with her.

"Don't be trying to get on with my woman, pops." Montrell said laughing.

"Act like it then before another nigga come and snatch her up with the quickness." Mr. Cole said to warn his son.

"She ain't going nowhere. I got this." Montrell said confidently.

"You so dumb and hardhead son, that girl not gone wait on you forever. You better get it together quick." Mr. Cole Said.

"Okay, I hear you, pops." Montrell said, not wanting to listen to his father words.

He knew Lashay wasn't going anywhere any time soon.

"Okay son, see you later. Mr. Cole said to his son, knowing he wouldn't listen to what he told him about Lashay.

"Bye pops," Montrell said, not knowing the advice his father just gave him was true and would later come back to bite him in the ass.

For the rest of the evening he enjoyed his time with his family and friends. He beat Lashay in a couple games of spades. They played other various games as well, told stories and shared old pictures from their child hood. It was cold that night in December and so much snow on the ground, at least six inches. All of them decided to all go outside and have a big snow ball fight. It was fun and hilarious. The kids had snow all over their head and bodies.

The Grown-ups were throwing it down each other coats, while wrestling in the snow. They all had a ball and were soaked when they were done.

By the time they left from his family's house, it was well after two a.m. They really did enjoy themselves and the time they spent together that night. Many more nights were filled being with each other and their families. From time to time they would hang out with each other's family without each other.

As time passed, Montrell always gave her money to get her hair and nails done or whatever else she wanted, but their time was always cut short and that got on her nerves. Montell never spent more than a few hours with her in a day. That would be the only thing they would argue about. He always told her he was working. Now Lashay was naïve to some things, but she wasn't that slow. She knew that "trappin'" didn't last all day long.

The whole time they were together they never had sex. He was too small, the size of her pinky and couldn't stay hard. He was too big in weight, so that wasn't gone work anyways. He would always eat her out, and she loved it. The things he could do with his tongue were shameful, so she took in other measures to please herself. She had to get herself off one way or another.

Since he couldn't do it, her toys and movies would fix the problem for the time being.

Even though they were only friends, Lashay knew it was other females in the picture as well. One cold night in March, Lashay received a phone call at three in the morning. She had just rolled over in bed and was getting into a comfortable position to finish her dream about Trey Songz. She had the biggest crush on him.

Who the hell is this? Calling my phone in the middle of the night, I got class in the morning, Lashay thought to herself. Her touch screen phone at was ringing off the hook playing Beyoncé Love on Top song.

"Hello" Lashay said in a groggy voice.

"Hello is this Lashay?" The female caller asked.

"This Lashay, who is this?" Lashay asked while yawning.

"My name is Janay. Do you know Montrell?" Janay asked in a hostile voice.

"Yes, I know him, he is a friend of mine. Why?" Lashay said in an irate voice.

"Bitch, that's my man, stop calling him and texting him. We live together.

He won't be coming to see you tomorrow either, its family day." Janay said in a slurred drunken voice then laughed hysterically.

"I didn't know he had a woman, I been talking to him for a year now, and now you want to call me?" Lashay said as she laughed. "If he was your man like you claim, he wouldn't be all in my face every day, taking me out and lying to you about where he is."

I got some words for Montrell ass when I get off the phone with this ignorant ass ghetto hoe, Lashay thought.

"Like I said, don't call him no more." Janay said shouting.

"I'm not gonna stop talking to him because you told me to, when I get ready to stop talking to him, then I will. I'm going to continue to be friends with him until otherwise; I don't know what to tell you, boo. Montrell didn't tell me otherwise, so I'm gone do me, and you do you". Lashay said, laughing loudly into the phone.

"I'm thirty seven. He stays with me at my house and take care of me and my seven kids." Janay said in a sarcastic tone. "He pay all my bills, and my kids call him daddy, I just use him for his money.

I got me another boo on the side that fucks me right, and I get bread from him too."

Janay was drunk as fuck, drinking patron from the bottle as she began to have loose lips, and she was telling all her business.

"I don't give a fuck what he does for you and all them damn kids you got. You need to learn how to use a condom and get on some birth control." Lashay said to her.

What does a thirty seven year old woman want with a twenty six year old man? Nothing but money and dick. Where they do that at? Dumb bitches do dumb things, Lashay deliberated to herself.

"You are being so disrespectful calling my phone about him in the middle of the night. Leave me the hell alone and get off my line, trick. Stop calling and playing on my phone, I have better things to do then keep you entertained." Lashay said nastily into the phone with her face frowned up.

Janay hung up the phone after that, she felt dumb. Hell, she had no comeback after that one. Janay felt humiliated that she even called Lashay. Janay had snuck and got his phone when he went to sleep.

She saw all of their text messages and phone calls and pictures sent to each other.

She was jealous of the pretty young girl that just came from nowhere who was trying to take what was hers. She would be damned if she lost him to her. He was her come up, and she wasn't giving him up without a fight.

The next day after school, Lashay called Montrell to tell him about his woman calling her last night. When Lashay called Montrell, he denied it to the fullest at first, but after her constant questioning and drilling, he finally admitted to it. Montrell told Lashay that Janay was his girl, but they didn't stay together and that she was crazy.

He claimed that she knew too much about him and had evidence about him selling drugs. He said that she would go to the cops and snitch on him anytime, and he wasn't trying to go down no time soon. Montrell had too much at stake to lose; his family, his house, his truck, spot houses, etc., and a stash of some millions saved up. He was trying to be the next best thing in the city.

Even though he had a girl at home, Montrell loved Lashay and really wanted to be with her but the situation he was in held him back from doing so.

49

Montrell never had Lashay around drugs, period. He didn't want her to get caught up in that, so he never brought it around her or did any type of deals when she was present. He didn't want her seeing that side of him. She was too good of a person to be caught up in some bull shit because of him. He wasn't having it.

As time went on, they became inseparable, but Lashay got tired of Janay constantly playing on her phone, harassing her, trying to fight her and other things. No holidays or special occasions were being spent together. He wasn't answering Lashay's phone calls or texts. She felt like he was on some bullshit.

Lashay decided to leave him alone for a while until he got it together. She refused to keep playing the side chick. Montrell called Lashay for weeks, and she never answered his calls or texts.

Weeks turned into five months since he had seen or talked to her, and he missed her so much. In June on a scorching hot day, Lashay decided enough time had passed, and they could talk. She called him and they talked for hours catching each other up on the things that were going on in their lives. After that, they began talking again daily.

Even though they talked, Lashay still wasn't ready to see Montrell yet. On the fourth of July, Lashay decided to finally see him that night. She spent all day with her family eating barbeque and having a good time. Montrell came to get Lashay about ten o' clock that night. They went to a hotel room and chilled out.

"Montrell we need to talk." Lashay said as she was sitting on the bed watching T.V.

"What's on your mind?" Montrell asked Lashay, with a confused look on his face.

He had no idea what she wanted to talk to him about.

"I know we've had our ups and downs, and I do love and care about you, but I don't know how much longer I can take this. You got too much going on that you need to straighten out with Janay first, before we could ever talk again. The bullshit and the games are done. I will not keep waiting on you to make up your mind about who you want to be with. So I'm leaving you alone for a minute." Lashay said, trying to hold back the tears that were welling up in her eyes.

"I can't even blame you for feeling that way; I fucked up bad with you." Montrell finally admitted, feeling like shit.

He was losing the best thing that ever happened to him. He felt like he couldn't breathe. The walls were closing in. Now he finally knew it was over between them. If only I had gotten my shit together, we would be together now and wouldn't be going through this shit, he thought to himself.

"Montrell are you ok?" Lashay asked, looking at the spaced out look on his face.

"Yeah, I'm good. No matter what happens, just know that I love you, and I'm sorry things turned out the way they did. I'm here for you if you ever need anything. I apologize sincerely from the bottom of my heart for getting you caught up with Janay. It's just that I'm in a fucked up situation that I'm trying hard to get out of. If she didn't know so much about me and what I have done, then I would have been left her alone. But, the thing is, I know that the slightest argument with her would have the boys knockin at my door, and I can't afford that ma." Montrell expressed. "Even though I never told you ma, in my eyes, we were together.

52

My biggest regret out of all this is that I didn't treat you right. I hope one day we can work it out. I love you!" Montrell said sadly, all in his feelings.

"You never know what can happen with us one day, but it ain't gone happen right now. I don't feel the way I use to feel about you. You really hurt me and made me wish that I never met you at all. You fucked up, not me. I gave you chance after chance, and you blew it. That was on you. What you won't do, another man will. There is nothing you can say or do to make me change my mind about you right now." Lashay said coldly.

She was so over him at the moment, but he would always have a place in her heart.

"That's fucked up how you feel, but all I can do is accept it, even though I don't like it. If I could take it all back and change things I would, I never meant to hurt you." Montrell said in a somber tone.

"Save it, I don't want to hear the same lies over and over again, you may be sincere, but I don't believe you. You have put me through so much in the last two years. I can't deal with it. I wash my hands of you. I can't keep trying to make you want to be with me.

If you love me and really wanted to be with me like you claim, it would have been happened a long time ago. I got to move on." Lashay said, feeling relived she finally got it off her chest.

She had been holding it in for a while now.

"I will give you your space, but you will not be out of my life," Montrell said. "If I can't have you, no one else could either. I ain't ready to let you go yet."

"Boy, you are crazy." Lashay said, while laughing.

"I'm for real. Think I'm playing if you want to. Don't make me fuck nobody up." Montrell said.

"Whatever Montrell, you ain't gone do shit. Boy please, you got me fucked up thinking I'm about to keep waiting around for your ass, I don't think so, boo." Lashay said loudly.

"You heard what I said." Montrell said in a matter a fact tone, not liking what she had said and how she said it.

"You gone get your feelings hurt. Let's go our separate ways, and if it's meant for us to talk to each other again we will. You will always be my friend." Lashay said.

"Friend my ass, its more than that, and you know it." Montrell said, filled with rage.

"It's time to let it go." Lashay said, knowing it was going to be hard walking away from him.

"I want you to be happy. Even if its' not with me." Montrell said, as he was thinking that he would never let that happen.

Lashay would always be his, whether she knew it or not!

"Thanks. It means a lot to me coming from you." Lashay said, although in her mind she knew he was lying.

"You're welcome, I love you." Montrell said sincerely, he had a feeling this would be the last time he would see her for a while.

"I love you too, friend, be careful out there. I have been having bad dreams about you. That you were shot by someone you knew, and that you went to jail." Lashay said sadly.

She wanted him to stop selling drugs and go to school, like they had talked about. She had a feeling something bad was going to happen.

"Don't talk like that, nothing is gone happen to me. I'm good, but you got a nigga lost ma! How you just gone break a nigga heart like that then tell me about a dream like that?" Montrell said, as he looked at Lashay confused and amazed at the same time.

He just couldn't understand her at times.

"Okay, if you think so, just be careful and please don't get yourself in nothing you can't get out of. You need to stop while you can. I don't want anything to happen to you." Lashay said apprehensively, in a warning tone.

"I hear you ma, but trust me I'm good this way!" Montrell said, as he thought about what Lashay said.

"Let's go to sleep, I'm tired." Lashay said, rubbing her eyes and yarning.

"Aight ma that's cool, goodnight ma." Montrell said.

"Good night." Lashay said, as they laid there and just held each other until they fell asleep.

Lashay

"Montrell really is crazy to think I'm about to keep dealing with his and Janay's bullshit. I've had enough. He gets no more love from me. I'm so done and over the situation. If he had of told me the truth in the first place, we wouldn't be going through this now. Oh well, his loss. I'm moving on." Lashay said, venting to her aunt as the pigged out on the couch, watching What's Love Got To Do With It.

The next day, they talked some more and got some lunch. Then he took her home and that was the last time she saw him. She had been calling him for two weeks and got no answer. One of his family members called her and told her he went to jail. It was a month before she had heard from him. Montrell told her he was jail and didn't know when he was getting out. Months had passed, and they were writing letters back and forth. Lashay received a letter from him stating that he got ten years. He wouldn't tell her what for, but she knew it was for drugs.

It had to be a big bust, because nobody got that long for the small stuff. Lashay left him alone after that.

She wasn't waiting on anybody in jail. It wasn't worth it. But she would still write him from time to time. That was three years ago, now it was time to move on. She was done with all the heartache and pain.

No more broke guys that can't take her out to Chili's, they want to eat off the dollar menu from McDonald's and expect her to be cool with it. She understood sometimes if you don't have it but not all the time. Who does that? No more dealing with guys who just want to fuck all time; that shit was so aggravating. No more dealing with guys who don't do shit at all. They want to get high all day and be turned up off a bottle but don't want to get a job. It's such a turn off. I'm so over that. Lashay was tired of hood guys' period.

After Montrell went off to jail, his people did some digging on who could have possibly snitched on him or gave a tip to the boys. Come to find out it was a family friend. Her name was Veronica. Veronica was a young hood-rat around the way that would do or tell anything for a few dollars. Unknowingly, she told Montrell's business to the wrong person. The feds were watching him for a while, and once they got the plug, that was all he wrote.

A few days later, they made their move and everything went downhill. Veronica thought everything was smooth until someone paid her a visit one day. All of her teeth were removed painfully with a pair of pliers, and her tongue was cut out of her month with a saw. That was to prove that snitches got stitches and to never run your mouth. Veronica hasn't been the same ever since. Now she has to eat through a feeding tube. Her mind was gone, and she was not able to take care of herself anymore. She lived in nursing home where she could be taken care of properly.

Montrell

Damn, I fucked up big time, and I lost everything. All that hustling, and shit to show for it. Lashay tried to warn me, but I didn't listen. I hope one day she finds it in her heart to forgive me. "Once a good girl bad, she's gone forever. I gotta live with the fact I did her wrong forever." Jay Z's words popped in his head. "Well, all I can do now is hold on and ride this shit out. I hope when I get home she'll give me another chance. Whoever she's with, they better treat her right, she deserved it." Montrell wrote on his notepad before he headed to chow.

Moving on, Lashay would go on a few dates here and there, but the guys who she would go out with would always have a problem with her disability. Guys would use her to talk to her friends or just use her for sex. They knew they had no intentions of calling her. They constantly stood her up, women would try to fight over their man. They all made broken promises to her that wasn't kept, and every other thing you could think of. Guys would just treat her any type of way.

But she was allowing it to happen to herself. Lashay used to cry at night to herself, get depressed, and take her anger out on everybody around her. She didn't have the boyfriend she badly wanted. Wondering why this kept happening to her but did nothing to change it. It was the same thing over and over again.

This one guy she had been talking to for a few months claimed he didn't have a girlfriend. One day they were sitting at his apartment chilling after coming back from a comedy show at the Fox Theater. It was around seven o' clock p.m. when she heard the car alarm go off to her purple 2000 Neon. As she looked out the window, she saw her car go up into flames.

"My fucking car is on fire!" She shouted to her male friend running outside of the house as fast as she could.

She was glad she grabbed her cell phone off the table.

"Oh Shit! I didn't know she was gone come over tonight." He said, running behind her out the house.

"Hell no, I know you ass don't have no woman, that ain't what you told me you fucking liar." Lashay said, with an attitude.

"We were having some problems when I first met you. That's why I told you that. I didn't mean to lie to you, but I knew if I told you that I had a girl you wouldn't even talk to me." He said, stopping her from going to her car that was rising in flames.

"You a sorry motherfucka, I hope she leaves your no good ass." Lashay said to him.

She had learned her lesson of dealing with other women's man. She was good on him.

"So, you the bitch that's sleeping with my man?" A small light skin petite woman said, as she took a crow bar and busted out Lashay's car windows.

She had already sliced her tires and keyed her car all over.

"I'ma kick your ass, bitch, for fucking up my car. I'm calling the police on you. Your ass going to jail for destruction of property. I didn't know he had a woman. If I knew, I wouldn't never fucked with him." Lashay said, rushing up to the woman as she tried to bust out another window.

She walked up to her and punched her dead in her mouth with a hard blow making her mouth bleed instantly. She fell to the ground. Lashay had a disability, but she could fight.

She didn't have a problem with whopping anybody's ass if needed. She wasn't about to take shit from nobody, point blank, period. She wasn't a fighter, but she would get with you if she had to. This woman deserved it.

"I know the fuck you didn't just hit me in my mouth." The lady said, in disbelief as she got off the ground.

"You need to be checking you man, stupid hoe. You bitches kill me always wanting to fight a woman over y'all man that constantly cheats on you in the first place. He's the one who can't keep his dick in his pants. So he's the one who needs to get it together, not me. Sit the fuck down and have several seats." Lashay said, pissed off.

"Lose my number, you bum." Lashay shouted to him.

She ran up to the ground hitting Lashay with a powerful blow to the back of the head. It was on then. The both of them was throwing blows back and forth, pulling hair, scratching and kicking while ripping each other clothes off in the process. Lashay was so hyped, she pulled the girl's hair until the white meat showed on her scalp making her bleed all over. Lashay had her on the ground giving her the business. She was trying to fuck her up and break her bones at the same time. She had never been so angry in her life. She didn't know what came over her, but she blacked out and snapped.

She was so mad about her car. A person was recording this with their camera phone, planning to put this on YouTube, Vine, and World Star Hip-Hop. No one jumped in to stop them either.

They didn't want to get jumped trying to break them up. Somebody called the police. It was too much going on, and it needed to be stopped. The girl was desperately trying to get up, but Lashay wasn't having it. The woman threw in a few good blows that caused her head spin, but that still didn't stop her. She wouldn't let up on her. She was like a Pit Bull attacking her prey. They both were so caught up in fighting each other that they never heard the loud sirens as the police were pulling up in front of the house.

After finally breaking them up, the police got their individual statements, and they decided to take them both to jail. The police felt like both of them were in the wrong, even though the woman had destroyed her car. It was a Friday evening, so they wouldn't go before a judge until Monday. This was some bullshit Lashay thought, as they cuffed and put her in the car. When they arrived to the county jail, they made her strip butt naked from head to toe.

They gave her a uniform to put on after they searched her. She was so glad they had put her by herself. She did not want to become anybody's bitch in there.

Women were whistling at her, yelling out sexual obscenities to her, making her feel scared and uncomfortable. She wished she could turn around and go home. She spent the whole weekend in that nasty, dirty, infected cell and had no intentions of ever returning there again.

When Monday came around at eight o clock a.m., her case was called. After explaining what happened, the judge he let her go with a warning. She only had to pay ten percent of a five hundred dollar bond. He let her know that next time he wouldn't be so nice if she returned to his courtroom. She thanked him as the case came to a close. She also asked him what she had to do to file a claim against the woman who destroyed her car. He told her to take it up with her insurance company and they would settle it.

Shortly after she was released from jail, she had called her cousin, Porisha, to come pick her up as she was being released. Porisha bonded Lashay out and went back to the car to wait for her. As she stepped out of the building, her cousin was sitting there waiting in a 2011 Edge Crossover.

Lashay was so grateful to be going home. She made a promise to herself and God from that moment forward, she would change her life around.

Lashay

She gone learn today. That bitch fucked with the wrong one and got beat down. I'm not even mad. I just want a new car. She asked for that one. She wanted to see me act a fool, and that's what she got. Thank God they didn't press charges on me. I was so glad my cousin was able to come get me. The struggle was real, and I can't wait to get home and soak. These clothes are going straight to the trashcan. I ain't going back there no time soon. Bitch ass nigga didn't do shit, but it's all good, I'm cool on him too.

Six months later, Lashay had finally settled her case with the insurance company for her car. She had purchased her a new 2010 Grand Prix. She stopped talking to all of those no good guys and started to focus on herself. She could do bad all by herself and didn't need them to help. She learned that she did not need a man to go out and do things with.

Lashay began spending more time with her family, went on a road trip to Las Vegas, and started writing poetry. This was a part of her she never knew existed, but she liked it. She had even started to go to church on Sundays on a regular basis. God kept her sane and content.

She began to learn the value of her worth. If a guy couldn't treat her the way she deserved to be treated, then she had no room for him in her life. She wasn't looking for a man anymore. When it was meant to be, it would happen. She didn't have time for bullshit anymore. It was time to grow up. Maybe one day she would meet someone who would treat her like the queen that she is. Lashay was human like everyone else, and she was ready to find her prince charming.

Chapter 3 Chance Encounter

It was Saturday night, and everyone was sitting at home bored. Lashay, Lexi, and Milian all decided to go to a party at a club that the radio station WJLB (97.9) was announcing. It was one of the hottest parties of the year. Young Jeezy, 2 Chains, Big Sean, Lil Wayne, and Dope Boy Cash Out, just naming a few, would be in the building. They had to go and represent. It had been a long stressful week for the ladies, and everyone just wanted to unwind and have a good time. About nine-thirty that night, the ladies all decided to go to Lashay's house to get ready. Milian decided she was going to be the driver for tonight. She was the designated driver because she hardly ever drunk liquor. The ladies were deciding on what they were going to wear to the party tonight at Club Ice. Lashay turned on the radio to WJLB. "Bad Remix" by WALE and Rihanna, was playing. That was they shit. They all started singing the chorus loud and off key.

"Is it bad that I never made love, no I never did it, but I sure know how to fuck, I'll be your bad girl. I'll prove it to you.

I can't promise that I'll be good to you because I have some issues, I won't commit, no not having it but at least I can admit that I'll be bad to you to". They all sung.

"I'm ready to get turned up y'all." Lexi said.

"Y'all, we need to hurry up, the line probably wrapped around the block." Lashay said, while looking in her walk-in closet for something to wear.

She had already showered and shaved so all she had to do was get dressed.

"I will not be freezing to death trying to get in no damn party. Somebody go let us in, even if I got to work a little magic." Lexi said, as she laughed.

Grabbing her Caress Body Wash, razor, and towel, she headed to the shower.

"Can you keep your legs closed tonight? You gone have baby number three if you don't stop." Lashay asked while laughing and coughing, trying to catch her breath.

She knew how Lexi got down.

"Whatever, get your life, I'm good." Lexi said in Tamar Braxton voice.

"I am so shocked you ain't trying to get it in. Are you sick or something?" Millian asked in a sarcastic tone.

"Shut up, Millian. Yo stuck up ass can't handle the dick anyway." Lexi said, in an agitated tone while rolling her eyes at Millian.

Knowing how she could press Millian buttons, but she wasn't going there tonight.

"Fuck you Lexi." Milian said.

"Since y'all noisy asses want to be in my business so much. I started my damn period today. So I want be doing nothing for a week." Lexi said calmly.

"Too much information." Lashay said

"I'ma leave both of y'all in a minute if y'all don't come on." Millian said sitting in Lashay's big round oversized chair.

"We coming, don't rush us, beauty takes time." Lashay said, while flipping her hair.

"Yeah, yeah just get ready." Milian said.

Milian was twenty five years old. She was a pretty dark skin girl with a flawless complexion. She resembled Gabriel Union, the actress. She stood 5'7 with long legs. She was petite with thick curves, one hundred twenty pounds and wore a size seven. She had no kids, and lived in Westland in a condo. She had a 2008 Malibu. She had a master's degree in counseling.

She's working at the WIC office as a supervisor until she found a better job. That's how she met Lexi.

The women all decided on what they were going to wear. Lashay wore a gray Michael Kors long sleeved, low cut, v neck sweater dress. It looked good against her chocolate skin. She couldn't wear a bra with that kind of dress, so she put tape on her nipples so they wouldn't show; along with a lacy thong from Victoria secret.

It was hot, showing just the right amount of cleavage without over doing it. It came just above her knees. The back was crisscrossed and dipped low stopping just at the end of her back. She rocked it with a nude pair of stockings, with tall six inch stiletto heeled boots that she ordered online from Just Fab. The heeled boots were a light gray color with silver studs embedded on them. They came all the way up to the top of her thighs. For her accessories, she rocked a two karat heart pendent necklace, which she bought from Kay Jewelry store.

It was beautiful. Every time it hit the light, the reflection from the diamonds in it shined as it bounced off the wall.

Along with the necklace, she had the matching sterling silver heart charm bracelet and two and a half karat big heart studs for her earrings. Lashay put on her black leather quarter length pea coat with it. Her makeup was light and simple tonight. All she had on was neutral gray shadow, eye liner, and explicit lip gloss from the makeup line by MAC. Lexi put some curls in Lashay's hair that was in an up do. It was thirty five degrees that night. She wanted to stay as warm as possible. To complete her look, she grabbed her gray small purse she got from Dots.

Lexi rocked a pair of dark blue denim True Religion jeans with a matching off the shoulder light pink crop top that showed her silver belly-ring with the True Religion words written in gold lettering across the top. She copped it from her cousin who was a booster that worked at a clothing warehouse. Her boots were ankle length, caramel, four inch stilettos to match her outfit. The accessories she had consisted of a pair of cute gold hoops and a cute gold star necklace with silver rhinestones around it.

Lexi had on a light pink shadow and clear lip gloss. She didn't wear it too much. Lexi just went to the hair salon earlier today to get her short hair done in with red tipped spikes. She just wanted to be comfortable since it was that time of the month with for her. She wore her black short coat that she bought from TJ Maxx. She had a long strapped gold coach purse to complete her look.

Millian rocked a form fitting, cream colored dress. It had a peek-a-boo slit in the front of the dress showing the top part of her cleavage. Her dress stopped at her knees with cream fishnet stockings. She rocked her four karat studs in her ears and pulled her fourteen inch Brazilian Remy hair in a side ponytail.

Her makeup was a neutral gold eye shadow, black eyeliner, false eyes mascara, and Sephoria natural brown lip gloss, with a cream clutch from Betty Wright. She didn't like heels, so she had a pair of tall, flat, brown, thigh high boots. Her short leather brown jacket completed her look. Now it was time to roll out to the party. They took Malian's car. It was a fifteen minute drive to the club. Club Ice was located across the street from the sandwich shop downtown.

At eleven forty five P.M., they arrived at club Ice, and it was beyond crowded. The line was wrapped all the way around a block. They parked the car and walked to the front of the club, bypassing all the people who were standing in the ridiculously long line, and headed straight to the front of the line. They ignored all the rude stares and comments from hating women who was jealous of them.

"Who do those bitches think they are?" a woman in line said.

Their looks alone made all the men stare and gawk at them.

"They fine as hell. The one in the gray dress can get it, she got a fat ass." A man yelled to his friend.

The women just shook their heads as they made it to the bouncers in the front of the line.

"How are y'all beautiful ladies doing tonight?" The ugly bouncer said.

He looked like Flavor Flav with a gold grill in his mouth. He had on too much Cool Water Curve men cologne. He was wearing an out dated black suit like the man from the old movie The Mac. He tried to be young again with his old ass.

He thought he was still the man with the ladies. His time been ran out a long time ago. The moment had passed.

"We good, how are you?" Lashay said, while trying to hold her laugh in.

"I'm good, trying to get to know you young sexy thang." He was pointing at Lexi.

"Sorry, but I got a man." Lexi said in an annoyed tone, while avoiding eye contact with him.

"I can treat you better than he can, baby." The bouncer said, showing of all his thirty-two teeth in his gold grill smiling at Lexi.

"If he acts up, I know where to find you." Lexi said, as she winked and smiled at him.

"Can I get your number? We can talk when your man ain't around." He said, desperately, hoping that she would give him a chance.

"Give me your number, and I will call you." Lexi said, as she pulled out here phone, pretending to put his number in.

"Okay, pretty young thang, I will be waiting". He said excitedly; really thinking she was going to call him.

"Okay boo." Lexi said, pouring on the charm.

"Do we need our tickets?" Millian stepped in asking the bouncer trying to save Lexi.

"Naw, yall good, sexy." The bouncer said, licking his lips lustfully at the women.

"Yall, go ahead to V.I.P. section, I got yall covered." He said.

"Thanks" They all said in union.

As they walked in the club, the D.J. was hyping the crowed up playing Trey Songz "Ohh nana na". They were singing along to the song while walking over to the bar to get some drinks. Girls had on dresses that barely covered their asses. They were grinding and twerking all over dudes, like it would be the last time they danced at a club. Weaves were sweated out and looking tore up. Guys were posted on the wall and in the corners trying to get women numbers. It was hot and stuffy in there, but no one cared. The D.J. was playing hit after hit. He played everything from 2 Chains, Drake, Lil Wayne, Jay Z, Chris Brown, Big Sean, J.Cole, Kendrick Lamar and many more. A lot of celebrities came through to party for the night. Such as Big Sean, Dope Boy Cashout, Young Jeezy, Lil Wayne, and other local artists came to show their support. If you were somebody, you were there.

The party was jumping, and everybody was loving it. It was time to get turned up and have a good time. They even had a stage set up for strippers. Ballers and sponsors was making it rain tonight. It was money everywhere while the strippers danced to their theme song "Make it Rain Trick" by Travis Porter, a throwback joint. The bar was packed from one end to the other. Everybody was trying to get a drink. Dudes were trying to talk to her all night, but she didn't pay them any mind. She didn't come to meet anybody. She just wanted to enjoy their girl's night out.

"I wish we didn't have to wait in this long line." Lashay said.

"Girl, somebody will get us in a minute." Milian said.

She was beginning to get irritated, people kept bumping into her.

"Y'all is crazy. Have fun with that cuz I'm going to go mingle." Lexi said, heading off to the dance floor.

She wanted to enjoy herself tonight.

"That heiffa always ditchin' us." Lashay said, as she looked around to get one of the bartenders' attention.

"It's cool, she gone need us for something, and we gone leave her ass." Milian said while laughing.

"She sure will." Lashay said, getting distracted by the FINE bartender who kept stealing glances at her, he winked at her.

"Girl, do you see him? That man looks so good." Lashay asked Milian

"Who?" Millian asked, trying to figure out who she was talking about.

"The bartender standing right there in the left corner making drinks for a group of women." Lashay said, while eyeing him up and down seductively as she talked.

"OMG, I know you not about to talk to him, he a bartender. He don't got no money." Milian said, in Tamar Braxton voice.

"I just said he was fine, I don't want to talk to him. He is broke and probably still live at home with his mama. Ain't nobody got time for that." Lashay said, knowing she just lied to Milian.

She was very attracted to him, but he look like the playa type. He resembled her celebrity crush and dream boo, Trey Songz.

His name was Xavier. He was 6'5 inches tall, light skinned, with a low cut fade with waves. He was two hundred and twenty pounds of nothing but pure muscle and abs. He was a gym junkie. He stayed in the gym three times a week and tried to eat decent. He was twenty six years old and had one daughter that came with a crazy baby mama. He owned two night clubs, a restaurant along with a few Real estate properties. And he even owned shares in The Motor City Casino in Detroit.

Xavier had retired from the drug game a year ago. He knew that he couldn't do that forever. While he was in the game, he stacked his bread. He was sitting on millions and millions of dollars. He lived in Novi, in a gated community home complex. He had five different cars. A Maybach, Range Rover, BMW 750 and others. He was one of the biggest drug dealers in Detroit. He was the man, but he so was low key with his, you would never know it. Xavier never was the flashy type, and that's the way he preferred it to be. His motto was never let nobody know everything you got, cause its always somebody who wants what's yours and will do anything to have it.

Even though he had female friends and a few jump-offs, he was getting older and looking to settle down with someone.

"I feel you girl, you ain't gone be able to do that." Milian said.

"He sure is nice to look at." Lashay said, trying hard to be discrete as she looked at him.

Unknown to her, he had been watching her the whole time he was making drinks. He was about to go over there and see what's up with her. She was looking too good for him not to say anything to her. He didn't even know this woman, but he was intrigued by her presence.

Xavier knew if he didn't talk to her now someone else would. He was not about to pass her up, yeah, he saw she that she had a disability, but he didn't care. He wasn't shallow like most dudes were. He wanted to get to know her, he had to have her. He watched as his boy tried his hand but got turned down with the quickness.

Her looks and body alone had him on swoll. He had to adjust his self so his dick would stop jumping and calm down.

"Down Boy," he whispered to his self as he made as way over to where they were on the right side of the bar.

He was helping out his staff tonight. He didn't have shit else to do. He was filling in for one of the workers who called off today because they were sick, which didn't happen often. All of his employees got along with him great. They did their jobs as a team making everything run smoothly without any drama. He couldn't ask for nothing more.

Xavier came from a single home background. His mom worked hard as a nurse to provide for him the best way she knew how. She graduated with her Bachelors' degree in nursing from Wayne Community College. Most of the time he got what he wanted, but he always got everything he needed. She struggled with some things here and there but it was nothing major. There was always a roof over their heads and food in their stomachs.

They might have lived in the hood, but his mother didn't allow him to act any type of way. Years later she married a well off lawyer after the divorce from Xavier's father. They had moved out of the hood and into the suburbs.

He had a regular nine to five job, but it wasn't for him. He didn't have to work, he just chose to. All they wanted him to do was go to school to better his self. He was very smart, so he got his Bachelor's degree in Business, but Xavier couldn't let the hood go. The streets called him. Hustling didn't last forever, and he had a backup plan for retirement.

"What can I get yall beautiful ladies to drink?" Xavier said while smiling at Lashay, the whole time bobbing his head to Chris Brown Loyal Remix.

"I want a Purple Rain, make it strong please. " Lashay said, while smiling back at him.

"I got you ma". Xavier said, as he winked at her.

"I want a Martini on the rocks with salt stirred not shaken." Milian said, while checking out the dance floor, all the while making eye contact with someone from across the room.

"Ok I got it, y'all drinks coming right up." Xavier said, as he prepared to make their drinks.

The party was winding down, and the D.J. started playing oldies but goodies. Usher's "You make me wanna" bumped loudly through the speakers.

As he finished making their drinks he sat them down on the counter in front them.

"Here are y'all drinks, one Purple Rain and one Martini on the rocks." Xavier said, the whole time looking at Lashay as he spoke.

"Thank you." They said, in unison.

"You're welcome." Xavier said.

"How much do we owe you for the drinks?" Lashay asked.

"All of y'all drinks tonight is on me. Enjoy the rest of your night. Let me know if y'all need anything." Xavier said, while looking Lashay in the eyes.

"Thank you so much, we appreciate it." Lashay said, smiling at Xavier.

"No problem ma." Xavier said, while he turned to walk away.

"Wait! Well, at least let me leave you a tip for your generosity." Lashay said, pulling out an en dollar bill, trying to hand it to him.

"Don't insult me ma." Xavier said, pushing the money back in her hand.

"Girl, why are you still talking to him?" Milian said in an uppity tone.

"I wasn't talking to your rude ass, get the fuck on somewhere." Xavier said, annoyed with Milian.

Something about her was grimy, he didn't care for her now. He went back to making drinks and interacting with other customers who was still lined up.

"This nigga is trippin', I'm out." Milian said heatedly, gathering her things to leave.

"Milian how are you gone leave us here? We came here with yo ass." Lashay said instantly getting irritated.

She could kill her right now.

"You and Lexi will be ok, catch a cab home." Milian said, as she was walking towards the exit.

She was jealous of the fact that she didn't get any play that night. Lashay and Lexi got all of the attention.

"I can't believe this bitch, that's why I don't fuck with her like that." Lashay said angrily, walking towards the dance floor to find Lexi.

Lexi had finally come off the dance floor after dancing through ten songs straight. It was time for a break. She was tired and needed some water. On her way to the bar, she bumped into Lashay.

"Hey boo, I was just on my way over to you." Lexi said, wiping the sweat from her forehead with the back of her hand.

"That bitch, Milian, left us." Lashay said, smearing her nose at Milian as if she was there.

"She did what! That's bold and fucked up." Lexi said in disbelief.

She didn't think Milian would do something like that.

"She's just mad because the cute bartender was talking to me and not her with her hating ass." Lashay said, while shaking her head.

"Ummmmm ummmmm, that hoe out of order for that one." Lexi said, making a reminder in her head to cuss Milian out when she got home.

They finally reached the bar, and Lexi ordered a water. It was hot as hell in there. She thought she was going to pass out. Xavier took her order.

"Here go yo water, miss." Xavier said, pushing the water in front of Lexi.

The whole time he was staring a whole in the back of Lashay's head. Lashay wasn't paying the bartender any attention at the moment. She was busy texting on her phone trying to find them a way home.

"Thank you." Lexi said.

"You're welcome sweetie, what's wrong with your girl?" Xavier asked Lexi.

"Apparently, my friend, Milian, left us cause she got an attitude for whatever reason." Lexi said.

"That's some foul shit, it's too dangerous for y'all to be out here alone at night. Fuck her, I can take y'all home. Is that ok with y'all?" Xavier asked, in one breath.

"Yes! Thank you." Both ladies said at the same time.

"It's nothing, y'all ready?" Xavier asked, signaling for someone else to take his place.

"Yeah, we ready." Lashay said, happy to have a ride home.

It was too cold outside to be stranded. They walked outside from the club, it was freezing and raining. Could the night get any worse, Lashay thought.

"Stay right here. I'm going to get my car, don't move." Xavier said running in the rain to get the car.

"I'm glad I bought my Rove today." Xavier said, thinking about his 2014 new black Range Rover as he located his car in the crowded parking lot, where people were running all over the place, trying to get to their cars and out of the rain that was pouring down heavy.

He got in the car and drove back around to get them. As he pulled up in the front of the club, everybody wondered who that was in the new Range Rover that sat on twenty six inch chrome wheels. He honked the horn at the ladies to get their attention. He rolled down the window and told them to come on. They began walking to the car.

"Girl, I didn't know bartenders made money like that, I need to do that then." Lexi said to Lashay while laughing.

She didn't know how he could afford a brand new car on his salary. Bartenders didn't make a lot of money.

"Y'all was taking y'all sweet time in the rain." Xavier said laughing, looking at their messed up wet hair as they got in the car.

Lashay got in the front seat, while Lexi hopped in the back.

"Whatever, the rain won't kill us, but this cold weather might." Lashay said laughing, getting comfortable in the seat.

She was glad the heat was on full blast because they were freezing. They all started laughing, agreeing with her about the weather.

"You have a very nice truck." Lashay said to Xavier.

"Thanks ma." Xavier said, as he smiled at her. "What's your name? I have been talking to you all this time and don't even know you name."

"It's Lashay, what's yours?" Lashay asked him.

"My name is Xavier, beautiful." Xavier said.

"It's nice to meet you." Lashay said, as he grabbed her hand to shake it.

He never let her hand go. They were still in the same spot in front of the club. She was trying to get her hand out of his, but he wouldn't let it go. So she just gave up. Lexi was in her phone playing candy crush.

"Are y'all two love birds ready to go yet? I'm hungry and tired." Lexi said calmly, smiling at the two who were making a connection with each other.

"I'm hungry too." Lashay said. "I will make us something when we get to the crib."

"That's cool." Lexi said.

"Can I take yall to IHOP?" Xavier asked them.

He just wanted to spend some more time with her before he dropped them off.

"Yes, that sounds good. I'm hungry as hell." Lashay said, as her stomach growled loudly. "We can't be out for long; I'm going to work in the morning.

"Okay let's go." Xavier said, pulling off into the street traffic.

They arrived at the IHOP that was downtown fifteen minutes later. The line was so long. They weren't the only ones who were hungry. Inside one of the IHOP hostesses rushed to him immediately when she saw him. Xavier had connections everywhere. He was a stand up dude. He treated people with respect and kindness. He showed his generosity where ever he went. In return, they showed him love back. He came in there two times a week and tipped them very well. They were seated in a booth immediately.

"So, Miss Lashay, what would you like to eat?" Xavier asked Lashay, as they all looked over the menu.

"I want a Colorado omelet with a waffle." Lashay told him.

She had been having a craving for that.

"I want an omelet too," Lexi said, butting in their conversation.

"I think I'm getting turkey sausage links, hash browns, with waffles." Xavier said thinking of the good food he was about to eat.

"I wish they would hurry up and come take our order." Lashay said.

They had been waiting a good thirty minutes for someone to come and take their order.

"I know right, I'm ready to smash some food." Xavier said, getting irritated from waiting so long.

"My stomach touching my back I'm so hungry." Lexi said.

"I'll be right back y'all, I'm bout to go find somebody." Xavier said, as he was getting up from the table.

"Okay," they both said, as they watched him walk away.

His sex appeal and swag had all the women turning their heads to look at him, while getting cussed out by their boyfriends in the process.

"He's such a gentleman." Lexi said, as she kicked Lashay under the table to get her attention.

She was staring off into space.

"Oh my bad, yes he is." Lashay said, snapping out of her thoughts.

"What you over there thinking about?" Lexi asked her.

"Damn, you so nosey, all up in my business." Lashay said jokingly.

"That's my middle name, you know I want the scoop." Lexi said in a chuckle.

"Honestly girl, I'm ready to find love. I'm tired of being by myself. It's time for me to get back out there, but I'm scared of getting hurt again." Lashay said.

"I understand your hesitation." Lexi said thinking of her dealing with Montell for two years and how it left her heart broken into pieces afterwards. "Every guy is not the same. You won't know what will happen until you give someone a chance, hun.

You gotta learn to open up again, if you don't, you gone stay single." Lexi said, encouragingly.

Even though she had her own love problems, she genuinely wanted her friend to find someone that made her happy.

"I will work on it, but I'm not making any promises." Lashay said.

"You need to get to know Mr. Xavier with his fine ass. If you don't want him, I'll take him." Lexi said laughing.

"Bitch, please, I wish you would talk to him, he's off limits, hoe." Lashay said in a way to let Lexi know she was playing, but for real.

"Let me find out, you got a crush on Mr. Bartender." Lexi said.

"No, I don't, I just thinks he's cute." Lashay said, lying through her teeth.

She was attracted to him in the worse way. She wanted to get to know him but was afraid to admit it to herself.

"Umm hum, whateva, I know you do. Its written all over yo face." Lexi said, knowingly.

"Girl bye! I'm good on him." Lashay said, fronting.

"Don't sleep on him, he could be the one." Lexi said.

"I don't know about that one." Lashay said, unsurely.

"I'm not gone talk to him after tonight anyways. He probably got a girl at home or a crazy baby mama somewhere.

"Well, whoever he got at home must not be doing something right, cause he all up in yo face trying to get to know you miss I'm playing hard to get. You know he trying to holla at you, but you wanna play that role." Lexi said.

"I know he does, but if he wanna talk to me, he gotta come correct." Lashay said.

"You so damn mean." Lexi said shaking her head at her friend.

She was a tough cookie to break.

"I'm not mean, I just have standards." Lashay said.

Just as she finished her sentence Xavier had walked up to the table with the manger.

"Hello, my name is Darnell. I will personally be taking your order. I apologize for the long wait." Darnell said.

He felt bad they waited an hour with no service. All the staff was going to hear it from him tonight. He was pissed. He was a short fat bald man. He was 5'6 caramel complexion with brown eyes and a big round belly. He was wearing a blue tight dress shirt with a tie and black slacks.

"It doesn't make any sense how long we've been waiting for someone to take our order. This is horrible customer service. If I drove my own car, I woulda been left. You need to fix this." Lashay said to him.

"I apologize for that. Let me reassure we can fix this. What I can do is have your food out in about fifteen minutes, tops. Everyone's meal will be on the house." Darnell said trying to smooth things over with the angry customer, even though it was coming out of his pay check.

"Thank you." Lashay said.

"What are you having tonight?" Darnell asked.

They all repeated they orders to him. After everyone's order was done, he hurriedly went to go put it in for them. As the trio waited for their food to arrive, they began talking about how hot the party was tonight. The ladies did enjoy themselves despite Millian leaving them. It had been a while since they went out. Fifteen minutes later the food arrived, and they all ate until they couldn't eat anymore. They all were ready to go to sleep after that.

About three thirty a.m. they left IHOP, Xavier was getting directions from Lashay how to get to her house. They pulled up ten minutes later. She stayed in a nice apartment complex Xavier thought to himself. He thought she stayed in the Projects. She must be doing well for herself he thought. He smiled inwardly. He loved an independent chick.

"Thank you again for the food and the ride." Lashay said.

"I told you, I got you ma." Xavier said.

"I appreciate it." Lashay said.

"Anytime ma," Xavier said to her, looking in her eyes.

"It was nice meeting you, Xavier, thanks for everything, but I'm sleepy so I'm going in the house." Lexi said, fighting off a yawn and getting out of the car.

Lashay handed her over her keys to get in.

"Take care." Xavier said to her.

"You too." Lexi said, walking towards the door.

"Can I get your number?" Xavier asked Lashay.

"For what?" Lashay asked.

"Cause I want to get to know you ma." Xavier said.

"I will think about it." Lashay said.

"Alright ma, I'll tell you what, when you get ready, call me." He took her phone out her hand and punched his number in and saved it.

"If I feel like it I will." Lashay said, awaiting his reaction.

"I see you trying to be funny ma." Xavier said laughing.

"It is what it is." Lashay said.

"I'll take that for now, but if you don't call me soon I will find you." Xavier said, putting it all out there.

"Stalker." Lashay said, giving him a creeped-out look.

"No, never that ma, but I always get what I want." Xavier said, while rubbing the side of her face.

She was so beautiful to him.

"You can't have me, I'm not for sale." Lashay said.

"I want you, and I will have you, believe that." Xavier said.

"Maybe if someone else don't beat you to it." Lashay said loving the game she was playing.

"I'm not worried about no other nigga. I'ma show you better than I can tell you." Xavier said.

He was willing to prove to her that he wanted to get to know her better.

"We'll see if I decide to let you get to know me." Lashay said, not believing anything he was saying.

"Yes, we we'll see." Xavier said, with a smirk.

He knew she was playing hard to get, but he liked a challenge.

"Good night Xavier." Lashay said, pulling on the door handle to get out.

"Hold up ma, let me walk you to the door." He said turning off the ignition.

"Okay." Lashay said, waiting for him to come around to her.

They walked up the pathway to get her apartment. She lived on the first unit. It was too hard for her to get the stairs on the second level.

"This is it." Lashay said, stopping at the third door.

"Okay ma, get some sleep. I enjoyed your company." Xavier said, as he pulled her body close to his for a hug.

She smells so good, he thought to himself inhaling her scent of The Secret Wonderland perfume from Bath and Body Works.

"I enjoyed your company too." Lashay said.

She was speechless, she couldn't believe he grabbed her like that. It took her breath away. The physical attraction that both of them had to each other were crazy.

"Use my number and you can enjoy it even more." Xavier said smoothly.

"If I'm not too busy this week, I'll call you." Lashay said, knowing she wouldn't.

"Okay ma, I see how it is." Xavier knew he was going to have to pursue her to get her to talk to him.

He stood there and watched her open the door to go in.

"Alright, see you later."

She waved as she turned to go in the house. Closing the door behind her, it was four thirty in the morning, and she had to be the work at noon.

"It's something about her that's special. I need to get to know her. She feisty but we gone work on that." Xavier said out loud to himself about Lashay.

Xavier

Headed on the freeway to go home, Xavier pondered as he drove. Lashay is bad as hell. She is someone I would like to get to know. She is a little feisty but I like it. That shit turned a nigga on, for real. It's going to be a challenge getting her to talk to me, but I can handle it. She just don't know I'll fuck around and change her whole life for the better.

I never chase a woman, but this time I'll make an exception. She needs to stop being stubborn and give me a chance. Xavier let his thoughts about Lashay fill up to capacity as he pulled up in the driveway.

Lashay

Lashay recapped the night's events in head as her thoughts ran. Millian is wrong as hell for that shit. I can't stand her stuck up ass. She was doing the most. Why Lexi hang around her? I have not a clue. That's on her. I sure won't be dealing with that hoe. I'll be cordial and that's about it. I'll be keeping an eye on that one. Anyway, I hate to admit it, but I'm feeling Xavier fine ass. He seems to be alright, maybe I'll give him a call. Lashay's mind stop running just as she turned the key into her home.

As Lashay walked in, she heard Lexi cussing out somebody on the phone. She didn't know who it was, but she felt sorry for them. When Lexi was angry she went hard with no remorse. She went in her room to lay down until she had to get up.

"You foul for that shit you pulled earlier." Lexi said to Millian over the phone as the T.V, blared loudly, she was watching Martin.

"What you mean? I told her I was leaving. Y'all could have left with me when I left." Millian said, not feeling bad one bit.

"You just left us without any way for us to get home, anything could have happen to us. We gone leave yo ass next time, bitch." Lexi said, getting angry with her all over again.

"I see y'all made it home just fine." Milian said, in a sarcastic voice.

"Yes, we did make it home thanks to the nice bartender, Xavier." Lexi told her.

"I know she didn't talk to him. He's broke. He couldn't possibly afford to take her out nowhere. She can do better." Millian said.

"You are such a hater. You just mad cause he didn't want to talk to you." Lexi said.

"No, I don't want him."

Millian was lying, she wanted him to fuck her.

"You must think I'm dumb. I seen the way you was eyeing him when we first got there." Lexi said.

"Whatever, no I wasn't." Millian said getting loud.

"Whatever, Millian!" Lexi said shouting.

"What the hell do you know?" Millian asked, curious to see what she would say.

"Just know I know." Lexi said.

No other words were needed. Millian hung up the phone on her.

"Damn THOT." Lexi thought, as she hung up the phone.

Lexi

Wrapping her hair up to go to bed, Lexi replayed the conversation in her head as she thought to herself. Millian is just jealous because she didn't get any play tonight. She ain't never satisfied until she got what she wanted. Stop while you're ahead, you are trying too hard. Clearly a guy is not interested in you or he let it be known. You know that no man won't like that stuck up attitude you be giving them not one bit they let you know that off rip. I highly doubt you can change someone's mind.

You're trifling as fuck, you pushing up on any man that comes within your grasp just because they show you a little attention. You're more desperate than I thought. I'm about to stay away from her. She can't be trusted. Lexi laid in the bed thinking about the crazy situation until her eyes got heavy and went to sleep.

Millian

Across town after Millian got off the phone with Lexi, she took a quick shower. When she got out of the shower, she left her towel on and sat on her bed to air dry. She got her deodorant and lotion off the dresser. As she began to put on her lotion and deodorant, she started to get horny.

"Damn, I need some." She said to herself out loud.

Quickly, she rubbed the rest of her lotion all over her body in a sensual manner, heightening her arousal even more.

The covers were already pulled back so she laid back and pulled the drawer open from her night stand. She felt around in there until she found her Rabbit. It was clear and about nine inches long.

This wasn't the real thing, but this would have to do until she got it. Taking it out of the drawer, she cleaned it off with its special cleanser then she applied some KY Jelly lubricant.

Getting comfortable on the bed, she laid down completely with her legs spread wide open. She began to rub her clit in a fast motion with one hand while she teased her breast with the other hand, with one finger she flicked and pulled on her hard nipples, getting her wet even more than what she was. As she whimpered, a low moan escaped her mouth.

Removing her hand from her nipples her hand glazed across her flat belly as she reached her hot throbbing pussy. She got her toy that was laid next to her and began to insert it inch by inch. Her legs were folded all the way back in her chest the way she liked it. She pushed it in as far and deep as it would go. She was dripping wet with her own juices as it flowed down her thighs.

"Oh shit, yes" She said aloud. It felt so good to her. "Hummm yes fuck me, fuck me hard. Keep going, don't stop, don't stop." She said turning herself on. "Get all in this juicy pussy." She said thinking of a man fucking her with hard fast deep strokes.

Her pussy began to contract tightly around the plastic dick as she went in and out repeatedly, on the brink of an orgasm. She switched to the doggy style position.

Arching her back and spreading her legs a little, she stuck two fingers inside her and began to grind and thrust back and forth. The faster she went, the more she began to cum all over her fingers. She cried out in pleasure because it felt so good. But it wasn't enough, she wanted to ride it. Getting into the Cowgirl squatting position, she lifted up and down as she slammed on it numerous times. Moving in a circular motion as she played with her clit brought her to her final peak. She came so hard, all she was able to do was roll over on her side instantly dosed off.

After cleaning herself up, she sat on the couch thinking negative thoughts. Lashay is cute, but she ain't got shit on me. What the fuck do guys see in her disabled ass anyways?

She has a big ass and a cute face, but that's about it. She doesn't look better than me. I need to step my game up. I can't have her outdoing me. Dismissing her thoughts as she turned on an old episode of Martin, it wasn't long before it was her.

Chapter 4: Trying to get to you

A week had passed since Xavier saw or heard from Lashay. Lashay still hadn't called him. Xavier was persistent; he wasn't going to give up.

It had been a long stressful week at the hospital. Her boss had her doing extra work that wasn't in her job description. She wasn't complaining at all. She just was tired and over worked. Dealing with people all day could be physically and mentally exhausting. The last thing on her mind was calling Xavier. She did think about him from time to time, but she felt like if he really wanted to talk to her, he would find a way to talk to her. After all, she had his number, he didn't have hers.

Lashay decided to fill in for her co-worker, Bridget, that Sunday afternoon. She arrived at twelve and wasn't due to get off until seven at night. She was irritated that the day was moving slow and not many people came there that day. She was hungry and ready to go home. It was four p.m. and time for her lunch break. As she was deciding on what she wanted to eat, she saw Xavier walking through the door.

He looked so sexy today in his red Polo shirt with light blue Polo jeans and matching Polo gym shoes. He rocked a three karat screw-in earring in his left ear with a ten carat white and yellow diamond, white gold chain and a fresh haircut. He had on the Unforgiveable Cologne from Diddy. You could smell it in the air as he got closer to her desk. He was looking so good to her she began to get moist between her legs. She wanted to climb over the table and fuck him right on her desk. Lord, please give me strength, she thought to herself.

She was so glad she wore black today, so no one could see the wet spot on her pants. She had to get it together. This was not the time or the place. Snapping out of her daze, she wondered how he knew where she worked. She didn't tell him, and how did he know she would be here today? He walked up to her desk and stood in front of her.

"What are you doing here?" Lashay asked him, happy he came to see her although she wouldn't show it.

"Hey to you too ma, with yo rude ass… I came to see you." Xavier said, smiling.

Unknown to Lashay, he saw Lexi at Fair lane mall in Dearborn earlier, and she told him where he could find Lashay.

"Who said I wanted to see you?" Lashay said, with a smirk.

"Damn it's like that ma, I'm so hurt. I thought you missed me to like I missed you." Xavier said.

"Ain't nobody thinking about you." Lashay said, holding in her laughter.

"I can tell cause you sure haven't called me." Xavier said.

"I been busy, my bad." Lashay said.

"You been busy, my ass, but it's cool. I came to take you to lunch so you can't say no this time. I'm driving my car." Xavier said, pulling Lashay out of the chair, not giving her a chance to respond.

He pulled her in a long tight hug with a kiss on the check. He couldn't figure out how this young girl had him so gone and he barely knew her.

Giggling she said, "I have to tell my supervisor I'm gone out to lunch. Hold on."

Wiggling out of his embrace, Lashay left Xavier watching her walk down the hall into an office to inform her supervisor that she was leaving for lunch and would be back when her hour lunch break was over. Her supervisor gave her permission to go.

She grabbed her coat, and they walked outside. It was a beautiful sunny afternoon with a slight breeze.

They walked in the parking lot to Xavier's vehicle. Today he wanted to keep it simple and drive his 2014 Lincoln MLKS. He unlocked the door with his keyless remote and opened the door so Lashay could get in.

He walked around to the driver's side and got in the car. They both put on their seatbelts and pulled off down the street.

"What you want to eat, ma?" Xavier asked her.

"I want some Nicholas soul food." Lashay said thinking about their great honey barbeque wings as her mouth watered in anticipation.

"You know you gone be late coming back to work, right?" Xavier told her so she wouldn't be mad because it would take at least thirty minutes to get there depending on traffic.

"I'll just let my supervisor know I'll be a little late on our way back." Lashay said.

"Ok ma, I'll remind you." Xavier said looking at her.

He wanted to lean over the seat and kiss her soft lips, but he didn't want to get smacked in the face.

"Thanks." Lashay said, as Xavier approached the freeway.

They took the I75 freeway all the way there. Thirty minutes had passed, and Lashay only had until six p.m. and it was almost five now. She was definitely going to be late. As soon as they walked in, a hostess sat them down in a cozy booth in the back of the restaurant, away from everyone else, giving them a private intimate setting. Before the hostess walked away, she let them know that their waiter would be with them soon. They didn't have to wait long, in five minutes a waiter came to their table.

"How are y'all doing today? My name is Candice, and I'll be your server today." the waitress said, handing them both a menu.

"We good," they said in unison.

"That's good. What can I start yall off with?" Candice asked.

"A coke please." Lashay said, needing some caffeine in her system.

"I want a lemonade." Xavier said.

He wanted something sweet since he couldn't have her. I wonder how she tasted. I bet she probably tastes as good as she looks. That's not something he did often, but for some reason he wanted to do that to her. He could picture her sitting on face and riding his tongue until she came all over his face while screaming out his name.

He was getting aroused just from that thought alone, he thought to himself. Coming out of his freaky thoughts and trying to adjust his pants unnoticeably, so nobody could see his dick sticking straight up in the air poking through his jeans. He heard the waitress ask if they wanted anything else.

"No thanks. We just gone look over the menu for a few minutes." Xavier told the waitress.

She told him "okay" and walked away to give the two some privacy.

Lashay was in her own world playing the Subway Surfing game and read a text from her mom asking her to come over for dinner on Friday. She was so busy replying to the text message that she forgot where she was at and that Xavier was even there with her.

"I'm sorry for being rude that was my mom texting me." Lashay said to Xavier.

She felt bad being rude to him. That wasn't a good look.

"It's cool, as long as I have your attention now, ma." Xavier said to her.

"You have my undivided attention." Lashay said to him, with a smile.

"What you want to eat, ma?" Xavier asked her.

"I want the honey barbeque wings with yams, macaroni and cheese." Lashay said.

"That sounds good as fuck, ma. I think I'm getting the tilapia with collard greens, macaroni and cheese, and cornbread." Xavier said, as his stomach started growling at the thought of food.

He was starving. He had just smoked some kush on his way to see Lashay. He was high as hell and had the munchies.

113

"Okay, I might have to try some of yours." Lashay said to him.

"Who said I wanted to share with you, ma? You got you own food." Xavier stated laughing.

"I see how it is; don't be all in my plate when it come." Lashay told him, in a sarcastic tone.

"You a trip, ma. How you gone tell me what I can and can't do on our first date?" Xavier asked her.

"This is not a date, I only let you take me out to lunch because I was hungry, and you offered to feed me. I don't turn a free meal down." Lashay said coolly.

"Straight up it's like that. You been spinning me for the longest and when I finally get with you and take you out, that's what you tell me?" Xavier sat there shaking his head.

He couldn't believe her, bitches these days be on that tip. When you try to be nice to them, they dog you out, and if he cussed her out, he would be in the wrong. He wasn't the one for it. He liked her, but he wasn't gone kiss her ass to talk to her.

The waitress came to take both of their orders and let them know that that their food would be out shortly. As soon as she left they continued their conversation.

"I didn't mean it like that, but I wasn't informed that this was a date. I'm just looking for a friend, nothing serious." Lashay said sighing, knowing she wanted a relationship.

By the look longing look on her face, he could tell she wanted more than just a friend. He could tell she was putting up a front to keep from being hurt.

"Keep telling yoself that if that makes you feel better, ma." Xavier said being real with her.

Being in denial about things was one of the reasons why his last relationship failed. Closed mouths don't get fed, and that was real talk. You have to be honest with yourself first before you can be honest with someone else.

"Whatever, Xavier, you don't know me or what I been through." Lashay told him getting defensive, knowing what he said was true.

She did lie to herself to so she could feel better. She had endured too much pain over the years from guys who she thought was the one for her. But in return all she got was lies and heartache.

When she loved, she loved hard, and she didn't think she would make it through another heart break. It was too much for her to deal with. She wasn't trying to go that route again. She was going to take her time and really get to know someone before rushing into things.

"I know you bitter as hell, and whoever hurt you fucked over you bad." Xavier said knowing all too well about how a woman can be when she's bitter.

They would be angry all the time, hostile, man bashing, and doing the most all because they had a relationship with a no good nigga who didn't treat them right.

"I'm just tired of getting fucked over and not being treated right. Every guy that I've either liked or loved, hurt me. They would lie, cheat, or couldn't deal with my disability. Those three things I can't tolerate or won't allow myself to put up with ever again." Lashay said feeling exposed and vulnerable.

She was surprised at herself that she was opening up to him and talking about her past relationships.

"Let me tell you something right now ma, I don't know what kind of clowns you been dealing with, but I don't give a fuck about your disability at all.

I'm not one of these lame ass niggas out here that likes to use and abuse females and then exploit them like they nothing after they done got everything they wanted out of them. I don't care what no one says about you or they opinion of you. I like you for who you are. It's what's on the inside that counts, and I want to get to know the beautiful person I see that's sitting in front of me." He stopped to point at her heart. "All that other bull shit you mentioned about being lied to and cheated on is irrelevant. If I was to cheat on you, I would break up with you first. That's just the type of nigga I am. Ain't no point of lying because your lies always catch up to you. The person gone find out anyway. So it's no point of doing that." He said, with a big smile on his face as he winked at her, making her blush in return and feeling special.

"It's not all about the physical with me. Yeah, you look good as fuck, and I would've fucked the shit out of you if given the opportunity if I met you a while back. I would've did that, but I'm not on that no more." Xavier said, keeping it one hunnit with her.

Lashay just sat there in the booth across from him speechless. She was lost for words, she didn't expect him to say that to her. She never had a man be real with her like that before. It was like a shot with no chaser. At least she didn't have to doubt or question him accepting her disability or other things she didn't like anymore. He made it loud and clear that he was okay with it all. That alone had her thinking that maybe he could be what she was looking for.

Their food had finally arrived, and they both couldn't wait to dig in. While they ate they made conversation, getting to know each other. They discussed the basics such as hobbies, goals, likes and dislikes amongst other things. They got so wrapped up in talking to one another they didn't realize how much time had passed, and it was going on six o clock.

Lashay just shook her head at the time knowing she was late. She knew she would be in trouble when she got back. They were stuffed and couldn't move after all the food they had just consumed.

"I'm late. I need to call them and let them know I'm on my way back." Lashay said, picking up her phone while searching through the contacts to find her supervisor number.

"Call in and hang out with me for the rest of the day." Xavier said to her, making her look up at him as he spoke.

"I can't do that, it's too late to call, and I need the extra money." Lashay said with a worried look on her face.

She knew she could be fired for this.

"I'll pay you for the day." Xavier said, knowing it would get her attention.

"You can't afford me for the day." Lashay said knowing damn well he couldn't afford it.

She had made an easy two hundred dollars doing overtime today. He was only a bartender, and they didn't make no real money, she thought.

"Try me, how much did you make today?" Xavier asked her.

"I made two hundred dollars today." Lashay said, awaiting his response.

"That's nothing, ma."

Xavier counted out five, one hundred dollar bills and handed it over to her.

"I can't accept your money, I'm good." Lashay said, pushing his money back in his hand.

She didn't want him to think she was a gold digger. She had her own money and didn't need his. She made more money than him anyways. At least that's what she thought.

"You offending me, ma, take it. You're the only female I know to ever turn down some money." Xavier laughed.

He pushed the money back in her hand. At least she ain't after a nigga's money, I love an independent chick, he thought to himself.

"Aint no man giving no money to a woman he just met for nothing." Lashay looked at Xavier sideways as she spoke. "They always want something in return. What's the catch with you? What you want?" Lashay asked him.

He had her fucked up if he thought for one second he was about to get some. Lashay didn't care how cute he was, it wasn't gone happen.

"I don't want shit from your stubborn ass. I can get pussy from anywhere, at any time." Xavier said, being real with her. "All I wanna do is spend some time with you and get to know you better. Can I do that?" Xavier asked her.

Xavier was getting real irritated and frustrated with her. She was putting him through the motions. Lashay sucked her teeth and let out a deep breath before responding. She wasn't trying to make him mad, but she was used to niggas coming on her the wrong way. So she stayed with her guard up.

"I guess I can be nice and give you a chance to become my friend, Mr. Bartender." She said to him, while she laughed.

"That's all I'm asking for, ma, is a chance to get to know you and become friends. Who knows what might happen, one day you might be my wife." Xavier said to her as he got up from his seat and walked over to her side of the booth.

Xavier sat down beside her. He pulled her close while throwing his arm around her shoulder. He turned her face directly towards his so he could give her direct eye contact as he spoke to her.

"We gone have to work on that smart as mouth of yours." Xavier said to her in a serious tone even though he loved her sassiness, but he would have never told her that for real.

"I'll try. I don't think I have a smart mouth. I just call it being real and expressing how I feel." Lashay said to him.

"Didn't yo momma ever teach you not to say everything that comes to your mind?" Xavier asked, while looking at Lashay.

This girl was something else.

"She always told me to speak how I feel within moderation. You can't go around just saying anything to people without no consideration for the feelings. That's how people teeth gets knocked out their mouths. Those were my mother's exact words to me." Lashay said.

He just shook his head and laughed at her. He could tell where she got her mouth from.

"Let me call my job before they fire me." She said to him as she dialed the number to her job.

When someone answered they transferred her to her supervisor's line.

"Hello," Ms. Johnson said as she picked up the phone.

"Hello Ms. Johnson, this is Lashay Jackson calling to let you know I won't be back in today, I'm not feeling well." Lashay started to fake cough. "Ugg ugg," she coughed. "I think it's something I ate, it's making me nauseous. I don't think I can make it through the rest of the shift." Lashay said into the phone to her.

"Okay, I'll get someone to cover for you. I hope you feel better, see you Tuesday."

Lashay rarely did take off, and if she was taking off something was definitely wrong, Ms. Johnson thought

Xavier was cracking up in his seat at the act that she was putting on. She turned around in the opposite direction away from him so she wouldn't start laughing too.

"Thanks so much, see you soon." Lashay said into the phone.

As she turned herself back around to face Xavier, she cracked a smile.

"Ok, bye," Ms. Johnson said hanging up the phone.

"Are you ready to go, ma?" Xavier asked her.

He was full as hell and had the 'itis and was ready to take a nap. Xavier didn't want to leave Lashay hanging. He really wanted to get to know her. He told her he wanted to get to know her, and that was his word.

Xavier didn't like telling people he was gone do something and not follow through with it. He felt like in this world, all you have is your word and your word is bond, and if you can't keep that, you don't have anything at all.

"Yes, I'm ready to go to sleep now." She said laughing.

Lashay than stood to put her coat on, Xavier stood to put his coat on as well. As the waitress walked passed them, Xavier requested the bill. She walked towards the back to retrieve it.

Lashay sat there wishing that the waitress would hurry up. All she wanted to do was go home, curl up on the couch with her favorite throw blanket and watch a movie on Netflix. They was too slow in here for her.

Ten minutes later, the waitress walked back up with a copy of the bill. She handed it over to Xavier.

Xavier looked down at the total of the bill pulling out a stack of money, counting out the amount of the bill along with her tip. The waitress' eyes lit up like dollar signs as she looked at his money.

This bitch right here. She couldn't stand a thirsty ass hoe. Lashay had watched her from the beginning peeping her whole game out.

"Here you go." Xavier said while handing over the money to the waitress.

"Thank you, enjoy your day." She said, trying to be discreet as she slipped a piece of paper in his hand with her cell phone number wrote down on it. Lashay saw it and was to outdone. Xavier just smiled at her grabbing Lashay by the hand and walking them towards the exit door. Xavier knew it would be a confrontation between the two and wanted to keep the peace. It was their first outing together, and he just wanted everything to be smooth.

He didn't want to give her any reason to stop talking to him. Lashay just held her tongue trying not to go there with him. Xavier knew Lashay would have a smart comment about ole girl.

This wasn't going to slide at all, Xavier thought as they walked through the parking lot towards his car.

"You ain't slick, I like that move you just pulled, I'ma have to try that one." Lashay laughed.

That was too funny. That waitress was outta order for that shit. She thought I was stupid and didn't see what she was doing. The things a female will do to get a man's attention are priceless. Females be too thirsty for me these days. She just shook her head in pity.

"Chill out ma, I'm not even interested in her. She can't do shit for me. I want you. That was some disrespectful ass shit she did though." Xavier said, to her as he unlocked the door for her to get in.

As she was adjusting her seat, he went around to the driver's side to get in.

"Whatever you say, Xavier," Lashay said, putting on her seat belt.

Xavier started the car up and put the radio on Hot 107.5. The hit song "Partition" by Beyoncé was playing. Both of them were bobbing they heads to the beat and pulled onto the street.

"You something else you know that." Xavier said, keeping his eyes on the road as he talked to her.

She was a piece of work. He wasn't feeling this attitude from her, real talk.

"Well, it must be something about me you like. Smart mouth and all, or you wouldn't be in my presence right now. You asked me out to eat, I didn't ask you, boo. Either you take it or leave it."

Xavier was irking her nerves to the fullest.

"Lashay, you need to check your attitude right now, ma, I ain't feeling it. You gone get yo lil feelings hurt. You don't have to be all extra with me like you be with these other niggas, who you have fucked with in the past, I'm not them, ma. Stop coming at me like I did something to you. That shit for the birds. Cause I ain't the one for that bullshit. I'm interested in you, so deal with it..." Xavier said, heading towards the I75 freeway again.

This girl was a trip already, and this was only the first date. He hoped she didn't act like this all the time. That wasn't attractive at all.

"Uggggh, well if my attitude bothers you so bad take me to get my car so I can go home." She said sarcastically while crossing her arms in front of her chest.

She didn't care anymore.

127

"You staying with me, I'm not taking you back to your car so you might as well cancel that idea and get comfortable. I'm taking you somewhere, it's a surprise, so just sit back and enjoy the ride." Xavier said.

Lashay was speechless, no words would come out. She couldn't believe he just checked her like that. Lashay began to look out the window, looking at the scenery as they drove on the freeway to their destination. Silence filled the car soon after. Lashay's body felt tired from all the running around she did all day, it finally caught up with her, and she fell asleep.

"I don't even know why I like her. If it was any other chick talking to me out of the side of their neck like they crazy, I woulda been dropped they ass with the quickness." Xavier said to himself as he glanced over at a sleeping Lashay.

She gave Xavier a feeling that he never felt before. The chemistry between the two was crazy. He didn't know what it was but it was a good thing, and he liked it.

Forty five minutes later, they pulled to Oasis Spa that was located in Ann Arbor, Michigan. This was his surprise to her.

Xavier just wanted to do something nice for her. He knew she probably could use one. He just wanted her to unwind, relax, and be stress free. Xavier could imagine by her having her disability, her body was in pain all the time and wanted to help. His mother has multiple sclerosis and had just found out recently. So he knew all about helping someone who was disabled.

That's why he didn't make fun of other people who were disabled. Since he was a little boy, his mother always taught him not to make fun of nobody, and if she found out he did, he got his ass beat, no questions asked. He saw her three times out of the week and hired a maid to help her around house and do other errands as well.

She took her meds daily, and that helped keep her going. She stayed active by participating in different activities, such as church, Bingo, concerts, and everything else you could think of. He wouldn't trade his mother for the world and was very grateful for the time he got to spend with her.

It had been a minute since Xavier had been here. The last time he came, he had brought his sister along. Xavier needed a good massage being that he was always on the go. He found a parking spot and cut off the car.

He didn't want to wake her up.

She was looking so peaceful sleeping. He hoped she didn't snap on him like some people did when being woken up from their sleep.

Letting out a long breath, he sighed gently shaking her, "Wake up, Lashay, we here, ma."

Lashay started to move from the sound of his voice, causing her to stir in her sleep. She didn't budge, she was knocked out.

"Shay, come on get up, ma." He said, shaking her on the leg with a little more force.

"Okay, I'm up."

Lashay was mad she had to get up, he interrupted her dream. She unbuckled her seatbelt and sat up as she looked around trying to figure out where they were at. She read the name on the building and immediately woke up. She was so excited to be here. This was her first time at a spa. She liked his style already and could get use to this. Her back and feet were killing her. He might just be a catch after all.

"Let's go in, ma," Xavier said, seeing the surprised but happy look on her face.

They both got out of the car and walked inside of the building. It was a few people in front of them, but the line wasn't bad. The line moved pretty quickly so the wait wasn't long. Five minutes later, they were called.

"I have a reservation today under the name Xavier Wright." He told the receptionist.

"Yes, I have you down for the 'Total Experience package, for two is that correct?"

"That's right." Xavier said.

"Okay, you're all set, have a wonderful time." The receptionist said smiling at them.

A male host escorted them down a long hallway to a room in the back where their massages would be taking place, giving both of them robes to change in. He let them know that the masseuses would be in there soon. They went to into the separate bathrooms to change. Ten minutes later, they both came out and really got a good look at the room.

It was so beautiful. The medium sized room was painted a cream color with green plants in the corners against the walls. Tall candles where lit everywhere on shelves giving it an intimate affect.

Along with two massage tables in the middle of the room with pillows and sheets on top of it, there was also a black love seat to sit on.

"This is so nice." Lashay said, looking around the room in amazement.

They both sat down on the massage tables across from each other.

"It's where I come to get my mind right and relax." Xavier said looking over at Lashay with seductive eyes.

She was looking real nice in that robe. All her curves were on display, and he liked the view.

"Look at you, over there checking me out." Lashay said, putting him on the spot.

"You sexy as hell, of course I'm gone look, ma."

Xavier was being honest. Any man was a fool not to try to talk to her, in his opinion. Baby girl was right, she had it going on.

"Thank you," she said blushing.

She felt shy at this moment for some reason. Maybe it had to do with the fact that her body was partially exposed in this thin material they called a robe.

"Anytime Beautiful." He said, flashing his pretty dimples, as he smiled at her.

This man looked too good for words. She wanted him in the worst way, but would never let him know it. Lashay was getting hot and bothered from his looks alone. She prayed that someone would come in the room right away. She was distracted by her nasty thoughts of him and needed something to cool her down. The knocking on the door caused her to jump out of her skin and come out of her thoughts. That scared the hell out of her. Xavier looked up her with raised eye brows wondering if she was ok.

"You good, ma?" Xavier asked making sure she was comfortable.

"I'm good." She replied, as the masseuses came in and introduced themselves to them.

It was a short petite woman and a tall muscular man. The woman would be working with Xavier, and of course the man would be giving her one.

They instructed them to lie down on their stomachs while they gave them a full body massage. It felt so good to Lashay, she began to dose off again.

Her body was in complete relax mode, and she enjoyed every single moment of it. There were few words exchanged between the two. They both were in their own zone. Soft Jazz music played in the background. They sipped on Champaign and ate a variety of fruit from a fruit tray. An hour later, it was time for Lashay to get a facial with a pedicure and manicure. Xavier just went into the sauna while she did her thing.

The body massage was all he wanted. His body felt rejuvenated and refreshed. All he was missing was a blunt of loud, but that would have to wait until later. It felt nice just to relax and not have to worry about anything for the moment.

Three hours later, they emerged from the spa. Xavier took Lashay back to her car so she could go home. He informed her that he was taking her out to dinner tonight, and he didn't want to hear any excuses on why she couldn't go. She agreed to go with him no problem. Lashay let him know if he stood her up, he was go have some problems from her. That was a big No-No in her book.

That's one thing that caused her to stop talking to a guy immediately. She felt like if he wasn't gone be able to come, he should be considerate and let her know, especially if she took the time out to get ready. She didn't play that. Lashay was starting to like his take charge attitude; it was sexy. Maybe she should open up a little and see what he's about.

Lashay got home around six-fifteen p.m. She had to hurry up and get ready. He would be there to get her at seven. She quickly undressed and went to turn on the shower, adjusting the temperature to her liking. She grabbed a towel from the linin closet and walked back in bathroom to get in the stand-up shower. Lashay loved her five setting removable shower head. It gave her the ability to use different options while showering. Fifteen minutes later she hopped out of the shower and went straight towards her closet.

She had no idea what to wear. As she was looking through her clothes, her phone chimed, alerting her she had a text message. She went to retrieve her phone from the night stand. It was a text from Xavier.

Xavier: I want you to dress in something nice tonight.

Lashay: I always dress nice. You don't know me well yet.

Xavier: u silly ma, that's what's up. Get dressed up but not overly dressed.

Lashay: ok I got you.

Xavier: See you soon.

Lashay: ok

Lashay went to her closet and found a one strap, pink, cute form fitting dress. She was wearing that along with black knee high panty hoes, with the matching lace bra and boy shorts from Victoria Secret, and tall, black, studded flat boots. She decided long silver oval-shaped earrings was all she needed. Lashay put on some pink eye shadow, eyeliner, and a soft tint pink lip gloss. Her hair was already flat ironed from earlier, so she just took the bonnet off and combed her hair down with her wig brush. She looked hot. She stood in the mirror and looked at herself for a few minutes. She was feeling herself, thinking, I'm a Bad Bitch. As she finished straightening up a little around the house, Xavier called and let her know he was ten minutes away. Lashay retrieved her pea coat from the closet, and as she was zipping it up, he rang the doorbell.

Lashay opened the door and locked eyes with Xavier. Xavier was looking good. He had on a black pair of slacks with a pink button up and a gray blazer, with black loafers.

He kept it simple with a pair of nerd glasses and an earring in his left ear. He was on his grown man tonight.

"You look stunning, ma," Xavier said, looking Lashay up and down.

Blushing and smiling she replied, "Thanks."

Xavier stepped closer in the door, reached out for Lashay's hand and pulled her out the apartment.

"We gone be late, ma," Xavier said, looking at his watch.

It was seven fifteen, and their reservation was for seven thirty five.

Xavier drove his black BMW 750. He helped her in then walked around to get in the car. He then pulled out of her apartment complex onto the main street. They were going to the Coach Insignia that was located in the Renaissance Center downtown. It was upscale and only by reservation. Quickly they arrived there with a few minutes to spare.

When they pulled up, the valet came to park the car. They got out of the car. Xavier handed over his keys along with a tip to the valet. Walking inside, they were asked the name of the party and were seated right away. Lashay thought the place was immaculate.
It had high ceilings, dim lighting and fine dinner ware. It had an amazing view of Detroit and Winsor. Their seats were in the corner by the window. They had a perfect view of the city. Lashay and Xavier sat across from one another.

"This place is nice."

Lashay wasn't about to admit to him that she had never been there before either. This place didn't fit in her budget.

"I'm glad you like it, ma, many people don't even know about this place." Xavier told her.

"I had no idea this restaurant was in here." Lashay said, glancing around the place.

"It's cool, ma, you gone go everywhere as long as you with me." Xavier said smiling.

"You so sure of yourself huh, how do you know if I'm going to talk to you?" asked Lashay.

"Kill all that nonsense." Xavier said.

He was starting to lose his patience with her. He was trying to be nice, but her attitude was so stank with him, and for the life of him he couldn't understand why.

"Do you sell drugs?" Lashay asked him.

He couldn't possibly get all those cars or take me all these places with his money.

"No ma, I got my own businesses. I own the club and some Real Estate Properties. I'm not a bartender." Xavier said, while laughing.

He couldn't believe she thought he was really a bartender. That was cute. She was fucking with a millionaire and didn't even know it.

"Well excuse me, I thought you were." Lashay said, while laughing.

"Never judge a book by its cover." Xavier said.

He would never admit to her that he sold drugs. He didn't want her to find out about that side of his life. At the same time, he knew if he got serious about her, he would eventually have to tell her.

"Ok, I will try." Lashay replied.

It was hard for her not to assume because that was what she was used to. She knew otherwise though. Lashay knew he wasn't straight legit.

Her woman's intuition told her so. Whatever is done in the dark will come to light.

They enjoyed a wonderful meal of filet mignon with garlic mashed potatoes and asparagus. It was delicious. The menus didn't have prices on them, so she knew it cost some bread for their meals. Followed by a few glasses of Chardonnay Wine, Xavier and Lashay was enjoying each other's company and getting to know one another. It was after ten o' clock when they left.

The date continued to go smoothly. They headed over to a Karaoke bar, where they sat and laughed at other people who were trying their hardest to sing the words to the songs being played all in a drunken slur. The two even got up on stage and did the Fire and Desire duet by Rick James and Tina Marie. They were just as bad as the people on stage. Neither could sing a lick but didn't care at all. Afterwards, Xavier took Lashay home.

Both of them stayed up all night talking and watching movies in the living room until the sunset rose. Shortly after, they fell asleep on the couch in each other's arms, dreaming about each other and what was to come next. There was no denying that they were into each other.

Lashay

Running her bath water, she thought of him. Damn, maybe I need to stop being mean to Xavier. He did surprise me today with lunch; that was very sweet. But I'm just scared to let someone new in. No, he isn't in my past, but it's just so hard to shake it off though. It really makes me wonder what his intentions are with me. Only time will tell if he's serious about getting to know me. I have zero tolerance for bullshit. I'm going to put my big girl panties on and give him a chance. So we'll see, he better act right. If not, it ain't nothing to cut him off. Lashay thought as she soaked in the hot water until it turned freezing cold. Shivering, she got out quickly and dreamt of the new possibilities.

Xavier

Puffing on a cigar, as he lied in his lay-z-boy, almost immediately, his thoughts went to the new woman in his life. Lashay has had a lot of fuck niggas and lames in her life. That had to be the only reason why she's giving me a hard time. She made me want to wring her neck today with them smart ass comments.

Damn, how many times a nigga had to say he's feeling you for you to get it? They say patience is a virtue, so I'm trying my hardest to be. Lashay better be worth all this trouble. If she lets me in, we will be working on that attitude of hers. I ain't the one for the games. There's always someone else who's willing and ready, believe that, Xavier thought, putting the rest of it out. He had a phone call to make.

Four months later, Xavier and Lashay were inseparable. You didn't see one without the other. Even though they hadn't made it official yet, it was apparent that they were really feeling each other a lot. Whether they wanted to admit it to themselves or not, their connection was like no other.

Chapter 5: Can't Let Go

"Oh shit, fuck me!" Keisha screamed out in pleasure as Juan was hitting it from the back doggie style in the middle of the living room.

He was all up in it. His long nine and a half long, thick dick felt so good inside her, all she could do was moan. He's bigger than that when he was all the way hard.

He had her bent over touching her toes as he fucked her with fast hard strokes. She tried not to lose her balance as her knees began to buckle as he began to hit her spot making her cum. This youngin had some skills and knew how to work that big dick of his, and she was enjoying every minute of it.

"You like this shit, bitch?" Juan said, pulling Keisha's hair hard, beating her pussy up.

"Right there, don't stop, it feels so good." Keisha responded, barely getting the words out.

"Take this dick," Juan said, smacking her on the ass as he went deeper inside of her, pounding away.

There were no words needed to be said. All she could do was take the dick as another orgasm began to build up as she came hard for the second time. All you could her were moans and grunts while their skin was slapping against each other.

He wanted her to get hers off first before he got his. He wasn't a selfish lover, and Keisha did have some good pussy. Her head game was on point too. That's why he been fucking around with her so long. If she didn't, he would have been left her alone.

"Ride this dick," he said.

Keisha got up and stood watching him as he walked over to the couch and sat down. As she was waiting on him, she was playing in her pussy and rubbing her clit in a circular motion getting wetter and wetter. She was horny as hell and ready to fuck some more. That was just a warm up, and now she was ready for the game. He pulled out a fresh Magnum condom and put it on his dick. He made sure it was on correctly, there would be no babies coming this way anytime soon, and plus, bitches were trifling these days. He wasn't trying to catch nothing.

He rather be safe than sorry. When he was finished putting on the condom, she climbed on top of him in reverse cowgirl position. She slid down his dick slowly taking him in inch by inch.

Damn, he was big, and she had to get used to it every time. Juan let her sit there for a minute so she could get adjusted to him. His big dick was no match for her, she could barely handle it. But she was horny as hell, she wasn't about to stop now. Later on, she would definitely pay for it. Keisha's small frame began to bounce up and down fast as she began to moan and say incoherent things to Juan. Her eyes began to roll in the back of her head. It felt good to Juan too.

Keisha's walls was tight and gushy, she had that wet wet. Juan wasn't one of those silent niggas when it came to sex. He liked to let you know how good it felt. He talked and moaned as much she did. Keisha was getting the job done. He was about to cum any minute now as his toes began to curl.

"I'm about to cum," Juan said, pulling out of her, peeling the condom off he began to jack his dick off, so he could cum all over her face.

"Okay baby," Keisha said walking over to him as she stuck her tongue out so he could cum in her mouth.

Getting on her knees, she crawled over to him.

"Ahh yeah, bitch, that's right, suck that dick, swallow this nut."

Positioning her head right in front of his dick while he stood by the couch, he fucked her face fast. She began to deep throat him without gagging. Her warm mouth felt so good to him he began to make an ugly fuck face as she glanced up and looked at him while caressing his balls.

He couldn't hold it any longer, without warning he came, not giving her a chance to be prepared for it. He pulled out and squirted nut all over her face, then she swallowed it like a pro. His cum was everywhere, all over her body, face and hair, but it was well worth it.

"Damn, boy, I'm tired as hell." Keisha said, getting up, walking to the bathroom to clean herself up and she had to pee.

She began to take a quick shower. All she wanted to do was lie down, she was sore as hell. Her kitty needed a break.

Keisha was pretty with flawless skin, the color of coffee with light green eyes, inherited from her mixed mom along with her pretty long brown hair. She stood 5'8", 140 pounds, C cup size breast and a handful of ass with curvy hips.

"A nigga need to chill for a minute, that shit was good though." he said, bumping into Keisha walking into her bedroom as she emerged from the bathroom.

He needed to get that one off. It had been a few weeks. He went to the bathroom, flushed the condom in the toilet and cleaned himself off with a soapy rag.

That was a good way to relieve some stress, now he could leave. She already knew what the deal was. He didn't cuddle up with these hoes. When you do that, they get too attached and start thinking you they man and shit. He wasn't that type. It was time to leave. As he was searching for his clothes, he located his pants in the corner by the wall. His phone began to vibrate loudly. He knew it was no other than his girlfriend.

If she knew what he was up to, she would have a fit and would be going ham on him. He promised her the other day that he was going to stop cheating on her and do right by her and the kids.

He didn't feel like arguing with her, so he just let the phone ring. He knew he needed to get his shit together, but it wasn't going to be today, but he did love her. She held a nigga down through everything. She would be dealt with later. For now, he just sent a quick text to her to pacify her for the time being.

To Wifey: I'm busy, I'll be home later I can't talk right now.

From Wifey: You better have your ass home before 1 am or I'm locking the door on that ass. You won't be getting up here, think I'm playing if you want to.

To Wifey: Cut the bullshit out, I said I'll get there when I get there.

From Wifey: Whatever, whoever the hoe is that you with, better let you stay at her crib. I'm tired of yo shit.

To Wifey: Yeah okay we'll see won't we!

Juan knew she was all talk and no action, or she would have been left. Just as he was putting his phone back in his pants pocket, Keisha walked in the room. She knew he was not texting that girl in her house. She wasn't stupid and wanted a little respect.

He could have talked to her some other time not in her presence. She didn't care, they was just friends, but she didn't like that at all.

She held her thoughts inside. She just rolled her eyes towards the ceiling and proceeded to walk over to her dresser to get a T-shirt and some panties to put on. Juan didn't say anything as he watched her dress. Keisha wasn't paying him any attention. She almost forgot he was there since he wasn't saying anything. Thick silence filled the room.

Deciding to finally speak, she cleared her throat and said, "Are you going to stare at me all day?"

"My bad, I wasn't trying to make you uncomfortable." Juan said.

She had a nice body, it wasn't too big or small, it was just right, the way he liked it. When he was a little boy he would watch his mother get dressed up to go out. He couldn't understand his fascination he had with it.

"You good, just stop being all weird and shit, staring at me." Keisha said, looking at him funny and wondering why he was staring at her while she was getting dressed.

She hoped he wasn't crazy in the head. They had been talking for a few minutes. This was the third time they fucked. She liked him, but he was young and had a girl at home. She had never seen her, but word on the street was she was crazy as hell. It didn't matter he had a girl, that didn't have nothing to do with her. As long as she was being taken care of, she could care less.

"I gotta make a run." Juan said, grabbing his keys off the top of the T.V., while putting his clothes on to go.

He just had to grab his coat from off the ledge of the couch that was in the living room. Juan was a cutie she had met at Chili's one night she had decided to go have a drink. He was six feet tall with caramel colored skin hair cut low with no facial hair. He was on the skinny side with a six pack with a pair of stunning piercing light brown eyes.

"Wait, I thought you was staying."

Keisha ran after him. She was on his heels. It wasn't about the money this time.

Turning to face her, Juan said, "It was cool chilling with you, but I gotta go. I might slide through later on."

He reached in his pocket and gave her two stacks. Reluctantly Keisha took the money from his hands. Now she felt used and cheap.

"Just let me know," she said hopelessly.

He was cool, and she did enjoy his company.

Juan gave her a quick hug and walked to the door. He never looked back as he walked out. He got in his 2014 Expedition and pulled off. Keisha just stood there in the doorway watching him drive away until he was out of sight. She closed the door, locked it and turned off the lights. Retreating back to her bedroom, she thought, this can't be life. She was tired of being alone.

Keisha's daughter, Laylah, her three year old, was gone with her daddy for the weekend. Keisha regretted the way she treated Xavier when they were together. They had met at a mutual friend's party and had been together ever since. He showered her with nothing but respect and love. She ain't had to work or lift a finger. Xavier provided her with things she wanted and needed. He didn't care what she did as long as she didn't cheat on him. They had been together for two years, and things were going great until one day Xavier told her he had to go out of town for a week to take care of some business.

He never discussed what he did with her. He kept his business and personal life separate. If anything was to happen, he never wanted her to be involved. He cared for her that much, and your woman can't know everything, that was like breaking the code.

Xavier was going to make a drop for a Jamaican cat in Miami and conduct more business with him. Xavier wanted to expand his product and keep moving up in the ranks. He never wanted to be a kingpin in Detroit, but shit, he was close to it. While he was away, she missed him. She got bored and lonely. Xavier ended up staying another week and half longer than he anticipated. Her friend, Tiny, came over one night, and they went to a club and got white girl wasted. Keisha was dancing and flirting with who she was dancing with. It was her intention to just dance with him and nothing more.

But he was telling her what she wanted to hear, and his touch felt good. She began to get turned on, and it was over after that. Xavier wasn't there, and she had needs. The guy began touching her in a sensual manor, and one thing lead to another, and they agreed to leave together and get a room.

Neither of them had a care in the world and wasn't being cautious of their surroundings and who could be watching. They had a one night stand, and one of Xavier workers just so happened to be at the club that night and saw whole thing.

When Xavier came back in town two weeks later, his worker let him know what was going on. Xavier couldn't believe what he heard. He was so distraught. The pictures he seen gave him all of the proof to confirm it. How could she do that to him? He had been nothing but faithful to her, and this how she repaid him? It was a wrap. That night when he got home, he confronted her, and she continued to play dumb with him. He let her know he knew what happened between her and ole boy while he was gone.

Keisha then broke down and told him the truth after he put it all out there. It was no point to keep denying it, when he knew the truth. What could she say? She had been caught, and there was no way of getting out of it. Xavier let her know right then and there, it was over. He couldn't deal with a cheater, he felt as though if she cheated on him once, she would do it again. There was no trust anymore.

Maybe if she had been woman enough to tell him what she did, they might have been able to work it out, but oh well, it wasn't meant to be.

Xavier moved out of their three bedroom apartment that they shared into his own two bedroom condo. He missed being around Laylah every day, but he would always get her every weekend to spend time with her. He loved his little princess with all his heart, and he wouldn't show her anything but the best. She deserved it. Just because her mother and him didn't work out, didn't mean that he wasn't going to be in her life or that she had to suffer because of them.

He was going to be in her life forever. Every girl needed their fathers in their lives, and he wasn't going to be a deadbeat. A real man always takes care of his kids. He definitely was going to show her the importance of being a good woman to that special someone when she got older. Xavier wanted to teach and show her the way she was supposed to be treated at all times. All he knew was that he wanted to show her a better example of how love was supposed to be, not what she had seen between her parents.

Kids remember everything, so he needed to do better. He didn't want her to think it was okay or acceptable. It had been a year and he could say he moved on. Xavier was glad Lashay came into his life. She made him feel better. He didn't know what was going to happen with them, but he hoped something good was going to come out of it.

Chapter 6: Taking a chance

Xavier wanted Lashay to meet his daughter, Laylah, for a while now. He felt like now was the right time. The two had been talking for a minute. They had great chemistry and a connection that was unexplainable. Lashay made him feel things he never felt before, and it scared him. He only knew her for a few months, but it felt like they knew each other for years. He knew she was special and could be the one. There were two people in his life that meant the world to him, his mother, Audrey, and Laylah. He needed their approval; if he had their approval of Lashay, that meant it was a good fit.

Xavier had been hurt before in the past and wasn't trying to go that route again. So he wanted to take his time to be sure that this is what he really wanted. If Lashay could get along with his daughter, treat her well and genuinely cares for her. She was definitely a keeper.

Laylah was his world, and he couldn't just have anyone around her, she had to be the real thing. All he had to do was talk things over with his mother about the situation. He knew talking to Keishia about introducing them would be a disaster.

He didn't fight women, but he was sure about one thing, it wouldn't even get as far completing his sentence with 'my girlfriend' in it before he would have his fingers around her neck choking her to death. He was not trying to be sitting up in a cell over-night, or period, because of his crazy baby mama. Keisha didn't want to see him with anyone. If she couldn't be with him then no one else could. He knew it was crazy, but it was the truth. She ran many women away with her crazy antics.

Xavier sat there in deep thought analyzing the situation, and all he could do was shake his head. The only person who could give him good advice and point him in the right direction was his mother, Audrey. He picked up his IPhone 5, went to his contacts and began to call his mother. Audrey was fifty years old with a caramel complexion, silky long brown hair, flawless skin, grey eyes. She was only 5'5" and still had a very nice shape. She could easily give the younger women a run for their money with her build. She wore a size ten and wore it well. She stayed in the gym three times a week to keep healthy and active as far her multiple sclerosis would allow her to do so. She was single but happy. Her second marriage resulted in divorce.

Her being so strong-willed, and independent, it drove her husband away. She retired from her nursing job at Beaumont Hospital of twenty-five years until her health got worse from the multiple sclerosis and began to slow her down. Audrey had found out she had it five years earlier and had been living with it ever since.

Xavier knew she was at home watching T.V., ringing three times before she picked up, she finally answered.

"Hello, Son," Audrey said, in an upbeat tone.

"Hey Ma, how are you doing today?" Xavier asked, in a laid back tone.

"Oh baby I'm good. How are you? What's wrong? I can hear it in your voice."

Audrey was rattling off questions back to back. She knew when something was wrong with her son, he couldn't fool her.

"Nothing Ma," Xavier Laughed.

"Whatever, now spill it," Audrey said in a demanding tone.

Xavier could picture her sitting there holding the phone and taping her foot on the ground lightly waiting on his response.

"Well, you know I been talking to Lashay for a while now." Xavier said.

"Yeah, it seems like you really like her, all you do is talk about her." Audrey said.

"I like her a lot, but she a handful." Xavier said chuckling as he thought of Lashay and her feisty ways.

His mother began laughing because she could picture a woman getting smart with Xavier.

"Humm, she must be something else." Audrey said joking.

Xavier got quiet again thinking of Lashay. Man, he had to get her out his head. Every time he thought of her, she brought a smile to his face. He knew he was really feeling her because he wanted them to become serious and meet Laylah. In this short period of time, he grew strong feelings for Lashay. Her presence alone had him intrigued. She was pretty, cool, funny, nice personality and had a great head on her shoulders, and she was going somewhere in life, what more could he ask for? He couldn't wait to hear her voice later, and wanted to see her. What the fuck am I doing? Only women do that shit, he thought to himself.

He was in awe of his self for day dreaming about her. Snapping out of his daze, he remembered his mother was on the phone talking to him.

"Boy, why you so quiet? That girl must have put something on you." Audrey said laughing.

That boy is whipped, she thought to herself.

Xavier was speechless. His mama was putting him on blast, he knew he had it bad but didn't want to admit it to himself. He just laughed.

"Mama, you a mess. Your mind always in the gutter." Xavier said as both began laughing.

"I'm just telling it like it is." Audrey said.

"I hear you, mama." Xavier said, still cracking up laughing.

"That girl got your nose wide open." Audrey said.

"Mama, I want Lashay to meet Laylah. Do you think it's a good idea?" Xavier asked.

"Now you know Keisha is going to be tripping. But I will tell you this; don't let Keisha destroy something good that you might have with Lashay." Audrey said.

"Ma, you know that girl drive me crazy. She doesn't want to see me with nobody." Xavier said, referring to Keisha.

"It was her loss." Audrey said, as she rolled her eyes to the ceiling, she couldn't stand that girl.

"She had a good thing, and she still wasn't satisfied." Xavier said, as he was reflecting back on his with relationship her.

It was all based on materialistic things, lies and mistrust. He was glad it over between them.

"She'll learn the hard way." Audrey said.

She thought to herself, these young kids don't have any sense at all. Don't never want the good thing when they have it, but when they break up, they want it back once they realize the grass ain't always green on the other side.

"That she will, if she hasn't learned anything yet." Xavier said, agreeing with his mother.

That was her problem, not his. He couldn't care less how she felt. Under no circumstances would he ever get back with Keisha.

"If you're serious about Lashay, then you need to introduce her to Laylah. They need to get to know each other. Children will tell you everything, especially if they like someone your with or not. Don't ignore things that Laylah might tell you, it can be true. Sometimes children can see things that we don't or don't want to see. Keep your ears, eyes, and mind alert at all times." Audrey said.

"Thanks Mama, you always know just what to say." Xavier said, happily taking in everything she just said.

"Oh baby, that comes from experiences in life and the lessons I've been taught. I only tell you things that I can relate to cause I been there before. The key to it is to learn from those mistakes and do better than before." Audrey said.

"You're absolutely right." Xavier said.

"Well baby, I'm getting off this phone. My show coming on." Audrey said.

"Alright, mama, go ahead, I'll call you later." Xavier said.

"I love you, and you better be here after church for Sunday dinner." Audrey said.

"I love you too, mama, you know I wouldn't miss it." Xavier said.

They both said goodbye to each other and hung up the phone. He made a note to himself to start talking to his mom more.

Xavier was going to get Laylah for the weekend, and he wanted to spend time with Lashay as well, so he was going to make it happen. He was excited to see the interaction between the two. He hoped everything went smoothly. If it didn't, he would have a lot to think about. Now the only problem was Keisha. He just was going to tell her what was up. It was no pointing of trying to hide his relationship with Lashay from her. She was going to find out anyway. He thought it would be best if he told her instead of hearing it from someone else. Then she would really flip. He knew she wouldn't like it, but she would get over it. It was about his happiness, not hers. She had her chance, now it's gone.

Later that night, Lashay called Xavier. She was busy all week and really hadn't had a chance to talk to him. She was missing her boo. She couldn't believe she was calling him that. Scared to admit her feelings for him, she tried to downplay the situation.

Even though she was in denial with herself about him, she really cared for him deeply and had strong feelings for him as well. She was slowly letting her guard down and was starting to let him in, but she was very cautious. She wasn't trying to get hurt again. That last heartbreak was horrible and she made it through that, but that was nothing she wanted to experience again no time soon. A woman's heart is like a vault, once you're in, you're in, and once you're out, you're out. There's no coming back. Shrugging off her thoughts, she dialed his number from her Galaxy 4.

Waiting for him to answer the phone, she wondered what he was doing. Four rings later, he answered.

"Hey babe." Xavier said, in a sleepy tone.

Yawning loudly, he excused his self. He was tired.

"Hey boo, how are you?" Lashay said, happy.

"I'm good. I miss you though." Xavier said sweetly.

"Is that right?" Lashay said.

"You already know I do, stop acting brand new." Xavier said, knowing damn well she was fronting.

164

"We gone have to fix that." Lashay said in a sexy tone.

"Are you going to come see me tonight?" Xavier said with a sneaky smirk on his face.

He wanted to see what she was going to say. He had something up his sleeve.

"Now, you know I gotta get up early for work." Lashay said.

"I know what time you have to be there." Xavier said, knowing he was about to get his way.

"At Eleven." Lashay said.

"I'll tell you what, I'll cook you breakfast in the morning and drive you to work in the morning." Xavier said.

"You ain't slick. You'll just want me to come back over there tomorrow after work, that's why you taking me to work." Lashay said laughing. "You ain't getting none either."

Lashay knew what Xavier was up to. They haven't had sex yet. The time was coming soon because she couldn't wait any longer, and she knew he was ready. She wanted it to be special between them. She didn't want to rush it and be disappointed.

"Chill ma. I ain't even on that, I just want to hold you." Xavier said.

"Sounds like a plan, I'm on my way." Lashay said.

Twenty five minutes later she arrived in her pajamas, which consisted of a tank top and pants. Walking up to the door, Lashay rang the doorbell. She waited patiently for Xavier to open the door. Xavier sat on the couch listening to Kissing On My Tattoos by August Alsina. He liked all types of music, but R&B was one of his favorites. As soon as he heard the doorbell, he answered the door. Opening the door, he just stood there and stared at Lashay. She was looking good in her pajamas. He wanted to rip her clothes off, pin her against the wall and give it to her right there. Yeah, he was on one.

"Hey Beautiful" Xavier said, stepping to the side to let her in.

Instantly he made her blush.

"Hey Love," Lashay said, bobbing her head to the song as the Testimony CD continued to play.

She liked the CD; it was hot. That was her second time hearing the CD, and she was feeling it.

She would definitely be getting it online soon. She walked up to Xavier hugging him and brushing up against his diamond chain. The scent of his Guilty Gucci Cologne made her woozy and was beginning to make her wet. It made her want him even more. Snapping away from her thoughts she realized Xavier was holding her tightly around the waist. They were enjoying the feel of one another.

Xavier finally pulled back. He was getting aroused and couldn't take it anymore. He grabbed the remote to his sound bar and hit a few buttons and Trey Songz "In The Middle" started to play. This was the perfect song that described their state of mind at the moment. It was time to get it in.

"Ma, are you ready for this?" Xavier asked kissing her bare shoulder blade.

"I'm ready!" said Lashay, smiling as she responded back nervously.

She had a need that needed to be filled, and only he could fill it.

"Okay, I hope so, cause once I get started, I'm not stopping." Xavier said seductively as he winked at her.

"I can show you better than I can tell you."
Lashay said.

"Let me see then." Xavier said smiling,
wondering what she was about to do.

He was harder than a brick.

Lashay didn't say anything else after that. From
this moment on, she wanted her actions to speak for her.
Looking over at him, she kissed him softly on the lips,
making her way toward his neck knowing that was his
spot. She went in for the kill as she made her mark to the
left side of his neck, where she began to lick, suck, and
kiss as she massaged his balls and played with him
through his jeans until she heard him moaning, and his
dick was literally poking out at her.

"Damn ma, you got me hard as fuck." Xavier said
stopping her immediately.

"Come here." Xavier said in a whisper, grabbing
her hand as he led her to his bedroom upstairs.

His bedroom was a huge room. It was beige with
a custom made California King Size bed in the center of
it. A big eighty inch flat screen was mounted on the wall.

Art pictures hung on the wall, and on his night stand, rested photos of him and his family, mostly his mother and Laylah. There was a cream love seat in the corner. Even his comforter was custom-made with his name written on it in a pretty handwriting. He had hardwood floors with special plush accent rugs throughout the room.

He gently laid her down and then proceeded to take off all her clothes. He began to kiss her passionately traveling down to her neck while biting and rubbing on her nipples, all the while whispering freaky thoughts in her ear. Lashay was in pleasure as he was doing this. You can call her a freak or whatever you wanted, but now she was ready to see what let loose and see what that mouth do. She was ready for her first oral transaction for the night. She was blunt with hers and wasn't afraid to admit she liked getting head.

Xavier knew she was hot and ready, rubbing her wet pussy that just seemed to be getting wetter by the second. He had a soaker. She was going to wet the bed. Her body was dripping like a faucet as he began to eat like a five course meal.

Taking his tongue, he spelled his name on it. She tasted sweet, like she'd been eating pineapples.

He knew he had a freak on his heads when she pushed his face all in it, screaming out and moaning, "Yes! Xavier, don't stop, right there," repeatedly.

As he opened her up, he blew on her clit. He just kept licking around and around, then circles. Licking her asshole made her lose all control. That sent her over the edge. He was glad she was clean. Everybody didn't get those privileges, and if that wasn't enough, he went back to her sweet center and began to fuck her with his tongue like it was his dick at a rapid speed. Her juices were flowing like a river down his chin. He hit her G-Spot repeatedly, making her squirt for the very first time.

Lashay's eyes rolled in the back of her head. This was the third time he was making her cum in less than thirty minutes. Xavier had some skills on him and then some. He wasn't stopping anytime soon. When she tried to get him to come back to her, he grabbed her hands and interlocked them with his so she couldn't move at all. She came another three times after that, and she was spent. She could barely move. Xavier just smiled. His mission had been accomplished.

"I know you ain't tapping out on me already." Xavier said.

"Ha Ha, you got jokes huh?" Lashay asked.

"You know yo ass is ready to go to sleep after that good nut." Xavier said laughing.

"I can't deal." Lashay said, as she cracked up at him laughing.

He was telling the truth though.

He climbed behind her and cuddled up next to her wrapping his arms around her waist. They laid there making small talk. Xavier gave her a good foot massage. Lashay decided to go get in the shower. She loved his massive bathroom, it had a big Jacuzzi tub and a standalone shower with a six-head shower head inside it, it was amazing. After the treatment and good head she just got, that was all she wrote. She was tired from the day's events. What a nice stress reliever. But she couldn't let him think she was going out like that. No honey, time for round two.

After she got out of the shower, it was on. Lashay grabbed a bar of her Goddess Caress soap and began to lather up her rag to wash her body. The soap smelt so good, she used it all the time.

She had this thing where she had to clean her body a few times before getting out. It was her only little ritual to make sure she was clean. Her shower wasn't complete without her Summer's Eve Feminine Hygiene wash she used every day. Her skin was sensitive, so she had to be careful using perfume soaps. Rinsing off for the last time, she saw Xavier walking in through the corner of her eye.

What is he doing in here, she thought to herself. Maybe he has to go to the bathroom or something. She had been in there a good twenty minutes, and he had to go. He couldn't wait a moment longer. He used the bathroom and washed his hands then he asked her could he join her in the shower. She agreed. Lashay felt cool air coming through the open door.

She turned her head and said to him, "Are you getting in?"

"What it look like?" Xavier asked.

"Smart ass, I just asked. Anyways, I don't want any company." Lashay said.

"Too bad, you don't have a choice. I'm not getting out." Xavier replied as he was thinking to himself, this girl is something else, this is my house, not hers.

I got something for her little ass though. She gone act right after this. He got in behind her. She stood to the side as he reached for his rag and body wash.

His choice of body wash was Dove Men. He cleaned his self. She was about to get out so he could have some privacy. As soon as she stepped out, he grabbed her arm with his soapy hand preventing her from leaving.

"Stay in here with me." Xavier said to her.

"For what?" Lashay asked.

"For this," Xavier said as he bent her over and slowly slid deeply inside her.

"Uhh umm," moaning, Lashay couldn't believe that she allowed him to do that.

It was so unexpected.

He braced his self as he went in and out of her. She was so tight and felt so good it made him want to cum. He could tell she hadn't been with anyone in a while. She had that snap back. She fit like a glove to his body. She didn't have time to prepare herself. She could feel it in her stomach, he was that deep, all up in it. Xavier began to increase his speed, smacking her on the ass, really getting into it. Lashay was on the verge of cumming as he began to talk to her seductively.

"You the shit," Xavier said, watching Lashay play with her clit as he pounded away inside her.

"Ohhh, yes, fuuuck, I'm bout to cum, baby."

She learned to never call a guy's name out during sex. That's how you got in trouble.

"This is mine now." Xavier said, becoming territorial.

He didn't want anybody else getting what was his.

"Yes, baby, it's yours." She responded.

Technically, it was hers, but for now, she would give in and stroke his ego. He was working with a monster. It was the length of his arm.

"Don't be giving my shit to nobody else." Xavier said beating it up, so he could get his point across to her.

She was hardheaded at times, so he had to let her know. He smacked her on the ass hard until it stung.

"I'm listening, baby, I hear you." Lashay said wincing in pain from the sting.

She got a burst of energy and was throwing it back at him with just as much as he was giving to her. Finally, he met his match.

She was going to be sore in the morning. It was a mixture of pleasure and pain in a good way, her body would thank her later.

Thrusting in and out, as she was nearing her orgasm, he came inside her. He didn't mean for it to happen quickly, but it did.
She had that good between her legs. They were so wrapped in the moment that they forgot to use a condom. Neither one of them was into having raw unprotected sex. At the time, it felt right. Next time, she would make sure they had plenty. She wasn't ready for no babies, or wasn't trying to catch nothing. Thank God, she took her birth control pills everyday faithfully.

They both washed up quickly and got out. She wrapped up in his towel soaking wet. Water was glistening down his eight-pack. His body was ripped to the T. Emerging back into the bedroom, Lashay sat in a chair next to the bed drying herself off. Trey Songz Anticipation CD came on, and Xavier put on "Scratching Me Up". And that's exactly what happened. Different types of positions were did, hair was pulled and sweated out, multiple orgasms, scratches, bites, and marks were put on each other's body all through the night.

They made love until the peak of the sun came through the windows. Xavier had fallen asleep buried deep inside her. Both of them had a very peaceful sleep.

Xavier

Lashay is smart, funny, and had a great personality. She got that good good in between her legs. A nigga got to be on point with her. I ain't trying to have no babies yet. If it did happen then we would be good. Lashay finally let her guard down and is slowly opening up. I'd be lying if I said I wasn't feeling her. She got me open. Lashay made a nigga work hard, no doubt. I just hope that all that wasn't for nothing. I really want to see where this is going. I really care for her playing hard to get ass.

Lashay

Love ain't always complicated. Over the last few months, Xavier has shown me the way I'm supposed to be treated and nothing less than the queen that I am. He respects me physically, mentally, emotionally and financially. He is having an effect on me in a good way.

I couldn't ask for a better person to be with or whatever this is. I'm not rushing anything at all. As long as he's good to me, nothing else matters. Last night, Xavier had me climbing the walls and then some. I thought he was going to break me in half. I handled mine and put it down. He won't be able to stay away. Xavier keeps laughing at me because I'm really limping now and can hardly walk. I was tender as hell, but the wait was worth it.

Chapter 7: Baby Momma Drama

One week later, Xavier called Lashay. She was on his mind a lot lately.

"Hey ma, what's good with you?" Xavier greeted her.

"Chilling, watching this show called, "Orange is the New Black"." Lashay told him.

"I heard that show is good." Xavier said.

"It is. You should check it out." Lashay said.

"I will one of these days." Xavier said.

"What you up to?" She asked, changing the subject.

"I'm chilling, getting ready to spend the weekend with my daughter. I would like to see you too. Are you going to come spend time with your man or what?" Xavier said.

"Ummm Humm," were the only words she could get out.

She was hesitant. This was a big step, and she didn't know if she was ready. At the same time, she knew eventually she would have to meet the little girl one day, just not this soon.

It wasn't a problem, but it would be an adjustment because she didn't have any kids and wasn't use to being around them like that. She would babysit sometimes, but that was about it.

Usually, she preferred not to date men with kids. Now-a-days, everybody had kids. So that wasn't really an option anymore. She was in no rush to do so. Babies cost too much, and not only that, she didn't have the patience for it. Xavier and his daughter was a packaged deal, and she would have to learn adapt. She liked kids but couldn't stand the baby mama drama that came with it.

"Baby?" Xavier called her name wanting to make sure she was still on the line.

She had gotten extremely quiet.

"Yeah, I'm here. I was just thinking about something." Lashay said.

"I thought yo ass hung up the phone. You know yo ass was thinking, 'awe hell nawl, I don't want to meet his daughter'." Xavier said jokingly, while laughing.

He knew this was a big deal and a huge step.

"You be giving me too much." Lashay said laughing, shaking her damn head.

She was thinking that but what never admit it out loud. "You know I'll come see you, boo." Lashay said.

"I have a question to ask you." Xavier said cutting her off.

"What's that?" Lashay asked him, knowing she already knew the question.

"Will you meet my daughter?" Xavier asked, letting out a nervous breathe.

"Yes, why wouldn't I?" Lashay asked, trying not to offend him.

"I just wanted to make sure you were okay with it." Xavier said.

"I would never have a problem with meeting your daughter or any other family member of yours. To me, that's a special privilege that not many people get. I must be special. And we not even together." Lashay said laughing.

"Something like that, bae. You should already know what it is." Xavier replied back coolly not wanting to let on his real feelings.

"I don't know; I could just be one of many." Lashay said knowing she wasn't going to get an answer from him, and she didn't want to appear jealous.

"I'm around the one I want to spend my time with." Xavier said sincerely.

Honestly, he didn't have time to be around anyone else and didn't want to be. He was into her. He was just going to have to show her that it was about her.

"Humm, we'll see." Lashay said.

"We sure will." Xavier replied.

"I'll see you later, sexy." Xavier said.

He couldn't believe he was on the phone caking like he was in high school again and was crushing on a girl. This was crazy.

"Alright, boo, talk to you later." Lashay said, as she hung up the phone.

■■■

Later that evening

Xavier drove to pick up Lashay from her house so they could go get his daughter, Laylah. Lashay was a little nervous and anxious to meet her. She hoped that Laylah would like her. She didn't want any drama between her and Keisha. Xavier had told her what happened between them and the reason for their break up.

He let it be known to Lashay there was no way they would ever get back together, and she didn't have anything to worry about. Even though she said okay, she would be watching and peeping everything out. She didn't put nothing past anybody. About fifteen minutes later, they got off the freeway, and shortly after, they arrived at Keisha's house. She stayed in Farmington Hills.

She had a nice three bedroom, two bathroom, two-story home. Xavier paid all the bills only because of Laylah. He didn't want her to go without anything. Outside of that, she didn't get shit extra. If Laylah needed anything, he would buy it himself and give it to her. There was no way he was going to give Keisha shit. He didn't give a flying fuck how she got it. She better get it how she lived. She fucked up a long time ago of him ever being nice to her.

They finally arrived to their destination. Xavier called Keisha on the phone, so she could bring Laylah out to the car. Hanging up the phone, he watched Lashay as she fussed with her hair and makeup. She was so prissy, she couldn't help it.

She was wearing a short flowing Maxxi dress and a turquoise halter-top. She looked cute. He began to rub up on her thigh.

"Xavier, what are you doing?" Lashay asked naughtily, knowing she liked every minute of it.

"I'm trying to get inside you." Xavier said.

"You're so nasty, acting all mannish." Lashay said.

"Stop fronting, you know you like it." Xavier said.

"You just want some tonight." Lashay said.

He be on that tip sometimes. He was a freak who liked to get it in anytime and anyplace.

"You right, but that ain't the only thing I want from you, ma." Xavier said, caressing her hand, looking into his eyes as he smiled.

He had a look in his eye that she couldn't describe. She could tell he cared for her.

"Aren't you laying it on thick," Lashay said.

"See man, every time I try to express my feelings to yo ass, you come with the bullshit." Xavier said, heated and very annoyed.

"I'm sorry, it's just that I'm so use to bullshit, that when I hear or see the truth, I have a hard time believing it." Lashay said, being honest with him.

"I hear you, ma." Xavier said trying to be understanding, but at times, his patience was starting to run thin.

Ole boy really did a number on her.

Xavier just reached over grabbing the back of her head and kissed her passionately. Keisha knocked on the car window making them break their kiss as they jumped. Forgetting where they were at, Xavier rolled down the window as he adjusted back into his seat. Looking out the window, he saw Laylah holding her hand.

Laylah had skin the color of cocoa. She was fairly tall for a three year old with long ponytails, deep dimples and a cute smile. She had pretty colored gray eyes like Xavier, high cheek bones, and a cute bell pepper nose. She loved clothes and everything pink. Her personality was one of a kind. She was a little diva in training.

"Who the fuck is this bitch?" Keisha said.

"Excuse me; I know you're not talking to me." Lashay asked.

"Who else would I be talking to? I don't see no other hood rats in here." Keisha said.

"Alright, alright, let's be adults and act civilized with each other. I don't have time for this bullshit today." Xavier said. "You trying to stand here and act all innocent like you don't be having other niggas around my daughter." Xavier said. "When have you ever known me to bring a woman or multiple females around Laylah?" Xavier asked Keisha, tired of wasting his breath with her.

Keisha just stood there looking dumb and stupid. Xavier has never brought anybody around. Lashay got out of the car to confront Keisha.

"Now, you can say whatever you want to say to my face. You don't have to send subliminal messages through him." Lashay said to her.

She didn't like Keisha already. This is why she didn't do females.

"I'm standing right here." Lashay said.

"Bitch, you barely standing."

Looking her up and down as she stared at her body, making a low blow.

Did this bitch say what I think she just said? I know she just didn't say that, Lashay thought to herself.

She broke out of her trance when she heard the following statement from Keisha's mouth, "So you about to let this handicapped ass bitch take care of my baby when she could hardly take care of her got damn self. What you Captain Save A Hoe now?" Keisha said, loudly enough so Xavier could hear.

She crossed the line and took it too far.

"No, let me." Lashay said to Xavier, stopping him in his tracks with the palm of her hand.

"Yeah? I maybe disabled, but I can take care of myself, thank you very much. At least I'm not sitting at home with my hand held out waiting for the next man or check to come." Lashay said.

"Fuck you." Keisha said. "Well, since you all up this crippled ass bitch ass, and shit, acting all in love, and shit, my daughter is staying here with me. You won't be seeing her for a while." Keisha said, trying to threaten him.

"Xavier, you better get her, she don't know me. The next time I ain't gonna be so nice, and my disabled, fucked up ass gone beat yo ass, how about that? "

186

Lashay said to her with so much venom in her voice, it sent a chill down her spine, scaring her.

She didn't say anything else to her, after she saw the deadly look in her eyes. She wasn't playing.

"We'll see, bitch." Keisha said, putting on a brave front.

"Don't play with me about my daughter. I'm telling you now, don't fuck with me. I'll send yo ass back to the projects so fast it'll make your head spin. Go on somewhere with that silly shit." Xavier said through clinched teeth.

He didn't want Laylah to hear him talk to her in that way.

"Do you understand me, Keisha?" Xavier asked with bass in voice.

She nodded her head quickly up and down.

"I'm out, man, my daughter is coming with me." Xavier said to Keisha as he walked up to the porch to get Laylah.

"Hey, daddy's baby, I'm sorry you had to see that. Are you ready to have some fun with daddy?" Xavier asked kissing her on the cheek.

"Daddy! Yes, I'm ready to go!" Laylah said, smiling really big and hugging him around the neck with her little hands.

"And Daddy, no more bad words, or you going to get a whopping." Laylah pointed her finger at him with her hand on her hip.

Laughing, Xavier replied, "Okay baby."

Keisha just watched them from the side while glaring over at Lashay, giving her the 'It ain't over look'. Lashay just shook her head as they drove off. Keisha was definitely a piece of work. It would take a miracle for them to get along. She wasn't equipped for this.

Lashay introduced herself to Laylah, and they were making small talk as they drove to The Cheesecake Factory in Twelve Oaks Mall. Xavier just sat back watching the interaction between the two. It was adorable. Laylah was telling Lashay about her favorite movie, "Frozen" and other Disney movies she enjoyed, her favorite things to do, and so forth. Lashay began to ponder and wonder what her child would be like when she decided to have one. Why in the world was she thinking that?

"Shay, are you listening? Hello?" Laylah said waving her hand back in forth in front of Layshay's face.

"I'm listening, Laylah." Lashay replied.

Xavier chimed in the conversation the rest of the way.

The line was wrapped around the block when they got there, so they went inside the mall and grabbed a few things as they waited.

Two hours later, their buzzer went off alerting them that their table was ready. They enjoyed their meals and had samples of different varieties of cheesecake. Lashay went to the restroom, and that was when Laylah decided to ask him some questions.

"Daddy, is that your girlfriend?" Laylah asked in the cutest voice.

"Yes. Shay is daddy's girlfriend. Is that okay?" Xavier said.

"She can be your girlfriend, Daddy, she's nice." Laylah said.

A few hours later, they went to CJ Berry Moore's. Laylah had a ball playing almost every game and lots of prizes. Lashay and Xavier were both bringing out their inner kid. Neither could ask for a better evening.

The whole weekend they bonded together, really getting to know each other. Lashay couldn't ask for anything better. She was definitely having a good time with Laylah and was looking forward to seeing her more often. Xavier's heart warmed that his two favorite girls were getting along with each other. He could get used to this.

Keisha

As soon as they pulled off Keisha went over a few houses down to her friend's house and told her what happened.

"Xavier didn't bring this handicapped ass bitch to my house. Is he going through something? Xavier is always going to be mine. Whatever thoughts she has about them being together, she can go ahead and cancel that. He's going to see what he's missing in due time. For now, I'll sit back and play my position. Trust and believe, bitch, this shit ain't hardly over. Xavier better not have my daughter around her either, or all hell is going to break loose. Lashay better watch her back." Keisha let out all in one breath.

"Girl, you are crazy. If you go to jail, I'm not bonding your ass out either." Raven said seriously.

190

"You supposed to be on my side." Keisha said angrily.

"Well, act like you have some sense, that's petty. I don't want to hear the rest." Raven said.

She was too grown for that.

"Fuck you! I guess you fickle today." Keisha said, as she stormed out.

Lashay

When she got a moment alone, Lashay texted Lexi with the quickness.

Lashay: Keisha is a crazy lunatic. I ain't going to be able to do that. Out of respect for Xavier, I didn't go there, but next time, it's going down. Why do people keep trying me? They just don't know I never claimed to be all the way sane. Xavier is going to have to put Keisha in her place, and that's all there is to it. If I do it, it's going to get real ugly and ignant. Control your bitches. Enough about her before my blood pressure goes up. Laylah is the cutest little girl and so well mannered. I like her. Xavier is really growing on me, that's my boo.

Lexi: Drama is in the air. And I am so happy for you!

She was excited and worried for her.

Lashay: I hope not if this keeps reoccurring, it's gone be some trouble.

Knowing it would be Lashay, she just didn't want it to get out of control.

Lexi: All I can tell you is talk to Xavier about that. He could be the one to nip it in the bud quick.

Lashay: Ok I'll talk to him about it.

When Xavier called, she expressed her concerns to him about Keisha. Xavier reassured her he would handle it, and that's what he did. She didn't know what was said between the two. Keisha didn't give her anymore problems for the time being. Things between them were going well.

Chapter 8: Bliss

Over the course of the months, Lashay and Xavier began to spend more time together. Three times out the week Lashay would come over and spend the night at Xavier's place and vice versa. Their feelings were intensifying for each other. But both of them still held back from one another, afraid of getting hurt from what happened in their previous relationships. They both knew if they didn't move forward with each other they could miss out on something great with one another.

Xavier lay in bed thinking of Lashay. She had just left for the day to go to work. He didn't want her to go. He even told her that he would pay her for the day she was going to work. What kind of man would he be if he allowed his woman to work? He didn't trick on no females. If you wasn't his woman, wasn't nothing coming your way. They say it ain't tricking if you got it. He just felt like it was his job as a man to make sure his woman was physically, mentally, and financially straight. If he had it, you had it, no further questions. Xavier didn't do it because he felt obligated; he did it because he wanted to. He was never stingy or selfish. He always looked out, that was just how he was.

Lashay refused to take money from him. She didn't want anything from him. She had her own money. He just didn't know it, and it wasn't his business to know, and she wouldn't tell him. She was always taught to never depend on a man for anything, especially when it came to money. Anything could happen, and she wouldn't allow herself to be without. She never expected all the things he did for her and more.

It was very thoughtful and sweet of him to do. Lashay would go out of her way as well to show Xavier he was appreciated too. She would do little things like cook him dinner, give him a massage, leave little notes around to make him smile, buy him trinkets as well as other things.

Xavier called his right hand man, Chandelor, to check on a package that was getting shipped to the connect. This was going to hold them for a minute. If everything ran smoothly, there would be sixty thousand dollars in their pockets, a piece, for a large shipment of some of the purest cocaine, molly, lean, ecstasy, and the highest quality Kush you could get. They had whatever you wanted, and if they didn't have it, they could get it. The fiends were going crazy over it.

Every drug they had stayed high in demand. Xavier just had to make sure everything was on point, or this could cost them a lot for a small mess up.

Dialing his number, Chandelor answered on the second ring.

"What up doe?" Xavier said.

"Shit, bouta put this work in." Chandelor said.

He referred to the drop that was going to be made.

"Bet, that's a plan. Don't stay up to long." Xavier said, his code words for 'don't fuck up or take too long with the transaction'.

"I got you." Chandelor said.

"Alright man." Xavier said, making a mental note to talk to him tomorrow.

"One." Chandelor said, as he hung up the phone.

Chandelor stood 6'2", 185 pounds of pure muscle. He was thirty-two years old, light skin, brown eyes, thick fine curly hair in a low cut. He resembled the actor Omar Hardwick. His body was muscular and ripped. Chandelor stayed in the gym regularly and ate right. He didn't do pork. He had his own barbershop, and was silent partners with Xavier in the companies he had.

They both had the drug game on lock in the D but planned to retire soon. He was growing tired of the lifestyle and wanted to move on to bigger and better things.

He had a little boy name Jacari. He was six years old and stayed with his mother, Denise, full time and visited Chandelor every weekend. He made sure to be very active in his child's life. He didn't have a father when he was growing up, so he wanted to do better. Chandelor and Denise had broken up years ago. He broke her heart. He was a play boy and wasn't ready for commitment. She couldn't deal with the cheating and consistent phone calls from the different women. She got fed up and called it quits. It took for him to lose her to realize what he had. Till this day, it was one of his regrets. She had been with him since the beginning. She never asked for much, just his time, and he could never give it to her. Chandelor let her go, and now she moved on with someone else who made her happy.

Now it was time for him to find someone to settle down with and call his own. He wasn't going to rush anything and just let it happen naturally when he did meet someone. He had it all, the nice house, cars, and a dog. He was just missing that one.

A few days later, Xavier and Chandelor met after the drop. They had to conduct business, so they met in a secret location on the west side where their office was held when business was involved. They never talked about things in public places. That's how people got caught slipping all the time. You never knew who was listening, or watching, for that matter. They was always cautious and careful. They worked too hard for the life they had. They had too much to risk losing over a little crack in the slips.

"What up, bruh?" Xavier asked.

"Nothing much, bruh, everything went smooth," Chandelor said.

"I knew I could count on you, you always get the job done." Xavier said.

Even though that was Xavier's best friend, he could never be too sure in the business. He made sure to have someone follow his every move and report back everything. That way, if something didn't go right, he knew who to go to. They didn't have any problems all this time, and he hoped it stayed that way.

Xavier didn't have many rules when it came to a drop. He just wanted the job done. If you got the job done correctly, you wouldn't have any problems. Don't cheat him or play with his money and his life, that's all he asked. When you got reckless, then that's when he would check you and put you in your place. Y'all would split the cost 50/50 and be on your separate ways. Yeah, he was retired from the game, but he still had a few loose strings to tie up.

Physically he wasn't there, but he was always in the background, and it was him who was on the line as well. His connect didn't trust nobody but him. He worked hard to establish a solid ground of business with them, and nobody was going to fuck that up. Because, in the end, he would be the one who had to answer to them. They didn't do too much talking or forgiving people for mistakes.

They stopped doing business with you completely, and you were laid out on a stretcher in a body bag. If he was going to pass the crown down to the next person in line, he had to make sure that they were right.

Not once did Chandelor mention to Xavier all the bumps in the road he faced getting the job done smoothly. Chandelor got pulled over by the police for speeding while riding dirty. If that already wasn't bad enough, he got robbed blind with a nine pointed to his head at a gas station for all of his cash and jewelry he had on him. He was thankful to still be alive, and nothing was missing or spilled. The product arrived on time. That would have really cost him his life. Chandelor knew if Xavier found out about any of this he would spaz out on him badly. He was taking that to the grave.

"You know I always got your back; loyalty over everything, remember?" Chandelor said, meaning every word.

He would never play Xavier. His loyalty always lied with him. Xavier looked out for him when no one else did and so much more. That was his brother no matter what.

"I know it, bruh, you don't even have to tell me, you show it to me time and time again." Xavier told him.

"It's nothing." Chandelor said.

"Fasho, you my bruh to the end," Xavier said becoming a little emotional causing his eyes to begin to water.

He quickly wiped them away so Chandelor couldn't see them. They had been through it all together. He couldn't ask for a better friend.

"We good, bruh, enough of this mushy shit." Chandelor said, laughing looking at him.

"Fuck you nigga, yo ass interrupting my moment." Xavier said, glancing at him through the corner of his eye, giving him the finger and laughing.

"Dog, you getting soft," Chandelor said.

"Never that. When have you ever known me to do that?" Xavier asked.

"Right, right....never." Chandelor replied as he reflected back trying to think of a time when something happened and Xavier displayed weakness.

What was funny, he couldn't think of one thing.

"Then that shouldn't have been said," Xavier said in serious tone, letting him know he wasn't playing.

Weak wasn't in his character, and he wouldn't allow anyone to speak as such.

"Chill bruh, it ain't that serious." Chandelor said, noticing the look he was giving him and feeling irritated instantly.

Damn, this nigga in his feelings right now, Chandelor thought to himself.

"As long as you know, we good." Xavier said, in a tone to let him know this conversation was over.

Silence filled the room. Nothing was left to be said.

Chandelor changed the subject to a lighter note. He kicked it with Xavier about how things were going between him and Lashay. He was very happy for his friend. He found someone who he was really feeling. He could hear it in his voice as he spoke about her, and see the look in his eyes that she could be the one. He wished him the best with his relationship and told him he thought Lashay was a good fit for him.

Xavier introduced Lashay to Chandelor when they were out one day shopping. They all went shopping and out to lunch with each other. That particular day, Lexi had decided to meet up with them for lunch.

They all began to get to know one another, and the friends grilled each one of them about their dealings and intentions with their friends. Both were very overprotective and didn't want to see them get hurt. They let each one of them know what would happened if something ever went down between them. Making it clear not to fuck each other over because they would be stuck dealing with the aftermath of the situation. Since that day, they all got along great.

The guys continued their evening, catching up on everything from current events, sports, and everything else men talked about. They ordered Thai food, had a few drinks and just relaxed. There were even a few matches of basketball played on the PlayStation 4. It didn't happen often, but when it did, they both enjoyed it. Time passed by quickly, and before they knew it, it was getting late and time to go home. Xavier went home got in the bed with Lashay. As he spooned up next to her, he fell in a deep sleep.

After a hard week of working, the weekend had quickly approached. Finally, it was Saturday. Lashay couldn't catch a break this week between work and her personal life.

Either it was someone with their hand out asking her for some money or putting her in the middle of family drama. Her cousin had just called her crying about her sorry baby daddy and his trifling ways for the millionth time already. Then had the nerve to ask for five hundred dollars, talking about the baby needs this and that like she's the father. She said she'd pay her back on the first of the month when she get her check. Lashay knew good and damn well she was not going to pay her back a dime. Lashay abruptly cut her cousin off in the middle of lame ass begging attempt.

"Michelle, I'm going to need you to have several seats and shut it down." Lashay said to her.

"Come on cuz, you know I'm good for it, I got you." Michelle told her hoping to get what she wanted.

"First of all, I am not your man." Lashay said. "Second of all, I don't have five hundred dollars, and if I did, you wouldn't be getting it. For the last time, I'm not Captain Save A Hoe." Lashay said angrily, letting her have it.

Michelle didn't say anything after that, she just hung up on her pissed off. She gone learn today.

She was pissed as she spoke her thoughts out loud, "People is really trying to take me there. I'm not listening to the drama and don't want to hear it or know what happened. It's always something going on. I am not made of money. What makes them think I have it more than they do? I work too hard for my money just to be giving it away. When will they realize I have my own bills to pay and have this thing called a life? When will enough be enough? And I'm always wrong when I say no or don't have it. If it was the other way around and me asking them, they wouldn't hesitate to say no, I don't have it or the other many excuses that they give why they can't. No more falling for the guilt trip or the pity card. I have to start changing things, or they're going to think they can continue to do it. They will not drive me crazy and stress me anymore trying to help or please them. The shit is getting old and played out, something has to give. Family is supposed to help each other and be there but only so much. If I keep allowing this to go on, I'll end being bitter and regretful. I love my family to death, but I have a life to live. No more negativity, and if I have to stay away from them, I would."

It felt good to finally get that off her chest, even though it was only to herself. Then her job was laying people off, and now her job is in jeopardy. She could be one of those people who received the pink slip and a tired rehearsed line of 'sorry we have to let you go because our company is making budget cuts'. She just wasn't prepared or feeling the idea of finding a new job. It was like she was caught in between a rock and a hard place. On one hand, she had some money saved up to last her a couple of months. But on the other hand, what would happen when she ran out of money or an emergency came about? There was no way in hell she was going to ask her parents or Xavier. She's going to figure something out.

"I need a drink." Lashay said headed into the kitchen reaching into the cabinet to get a shot glass.

After she retrieved it, she walked over to her mini bar in the dining room. It was stocked and filled to the max with a variety of different liquors. Humm, I wonder which one I'm going to have, she said in her mind. Patron it is. She filled her glass up to the rim, taking two shots to the head.

Now that I got my drink, Let me call Lexi, she thought. Picking up her phone off the counter she said into the phone, "Call Lexi."

As it dialed her number, Lexi picked up on the first ring.

"You done finally came up for air." Lexi answered.

Laughing before she spoke

"What you talking about?" Lashay asked, playing dumb.

"Girl, you been M.I.A. these days. What you been doing besides letting Xavier blow your back out."

"I haven't been doing anything, for your information." Lashay replied, lying through her teeth.

"Bye Lashay! Even you don't believe that. I haven't seen or heard from you in a month of Sundays. I know you been doing it, trying to act all innocent." Lexi said knowing her friend.

They both just busted out laughing. Lord knows she needed it, considering all that she had been going through. It's a welcoming distraction even if it lasted for a minute.

"Yeah, I been a little busy with Xavier." Lashay admitted.

"Tahh. That's putting it lightly." Lexi said, thinking of the numerous calls and texts she sent her.

She was beginning to actually miss her.

"Whatever, I know you missed me." Lashay said.

"You wish." Lexi said laughing.

"Umm hum." Lashay said, knowing she did.

"So tell me is Xavier packing?" Lexi said, getting to the dirt.

"Damn, you nosy as hell, but to answer your question, nosy, I have no complaints." Lashay said.

She wasn't about to go into detail about her man's size or anything else. When you tell a woman how your man is in the bedroom, they get curious and want to find out them self. Never kiss and tell. They'll be smiling in your face and fucking your man behind your back. So to prevent a trip to jail or the emergency room, she would say very little in that department.

"I can't be mad at that. It must've been good, yo ass all smiles. Are you glowing too?" Lexi said, completely understanding and joking with her friend.

She finally let someone dust the cobwebs off. She was happy for her.

"Girl, you ain't gone believe what happened." Lashay said changing the subject.

"What up?" Lexi asked.

"Tell me why Michelle ass called me a little while ago asking me can she borrow five hundred dollars!" Lashay said.

"Are you fucking kidding me?"

Lexi was to out done, and it wasn't even her. She felt like some of Lashay's family members were always trying to get over and milk her for what she had.

"You know I ain't lying." Lashay said.

"I already know." Lexi said shaking her head.

"And then my job is laying people off left and right. I might be out of a job soon. So I have to figure out something."

"I'll keep you in my prayers. God always makes a way." Lexi said encouragingly trying to uplift her friend.

"Yes he does. Thanks, I needed to hear that." Lashay said.

"You'll be happy to know I been working for a month now as a CNA at St. John Hospital on Mac and Morross."

"That's great!" Lashay said, proud her friend was finally moving in the right direction.

"How are my god daughters doing?" Lashay asked.

"Getting big and driving me crazy as usual." Lexi said.

"I have to come see them." Lashay said.

"Yes, they been asking about you." Lexi said

"Tell them next weekend I'm coming to get them."

Lashay thought it would be a good idea to introduce them to Laylah.

"I sure will."

Lexi could really use a break between work and being a parent. She was worn out.

"Alright," Lashay said.

"Let's go out tonight and let off some stress."

"Where we going?" Lashay asked.

"To Nikki's," Lexi said.

"That's right around the corner from me, I'm down." Lashay said.

"I'm going to come get you, don't be moving like molasses. Hurry up and get ready." Lexi said.

"When you get a car??" Lashay asked.

"Two weeks ago," Lexi said excitedly.

"Go head, boo," Lashay said.

"Thanks, now, I'll be there in thirty minutes. If yo ass ain't ready when I pull up, you'll be driving your damn self."

"Okay mama, I'll be ready, now get off my line." Lashay said.

"See you soon." Lexi said, as she hung up.

Lashay went inside her bedroom and began searching through her closet for something to wear.

"What I'm I going to put on?" She said.

She had a plain coral dress with the back out and a purple mini dress with the sides and back out, she had just got them a few days before at Forever Twenty One. She held them up to her in her full length mirror to see which one she wanted to go with.

"I'm feeling the purple. " Lashay said as she laid the dress across her bed.

She walked into the bathroom, turning on the shower as she got in. Lashay hoped out refreshed.

"Shit, let me hurry up before she be calling me." Lashay said, running backing into the bedroom as she quickly dried off her body.

She went to the dresser and got her matching set of her black strapless bra and thong. Five minutes later, she was completely dressed. Applying her Jergens Lotion on her body, her phone started going off. Is she outside already? Well, at least I'm dressed. Reaching on her pillow, she just answered right before it hung up.

"Come on out." Lexi said into the phone.

"I need you to help me put my hair up in a bun." Lashay said to her.

"I shoulda known." Lexi said Laughing.

Lexi walked in wearing a red long strapless maxi dress with heels. She looked very nice with her new bob she was rocking.

"Look at you all cute, Xavier gone kick yo ass when he see that short dress on you barely covering you."Lexi said.

"I'm grown, Xavier ain't gone do nothing, he ain't my daddy." Lashay said.

"Yeah, umm hum, we'll see."

"You get on my nerves." Lashay said.

"Don't get mad because I'm stating the facts."

"Whatever, now come on and fix my hair, so I can do my make-up please."

"Now you wanna rush somebody, you a trip." Lexi said laughing as the two walked in the bathroom to fix Lashay's hair.

Ten minutes later she was done, and Lashay was doing her make up.

"Lexi, can you find me some wedges to put on?"

"I got you." Lexi replied, walking to her closet to pick out a pair.

She settled on some silver wedges since Lashay's outfit is accented with silver. Lashay walked out the bathroom and got her purple blazer from the closet and her purse off the bed. They left out the door after setting the alarm. Lexi had a 2004 Grand Prix, and she was loving it. It felt good having her own.

Shortly after, they pulled up to the club. Surprisingly, they found a decent parking spot.

As soon as they were approaching the long line, the bouncer recognized them right away and let them in with no hesitation. They went straight to the grown and sexy side. Walking up to the bar, Lashay ordered a drink called Tap That Ass, and Lexi had a Sex On The Beach. After the first drink, they headed to the dance floor and began dancing to a song called "Circle" by Little Ronny, and Paranoid Remix by T Dollaz.

The crowd began getting hyped. Weaves were sweated out, clothes were barely visible, bodies were touching, you could hardly move. Dancing through six songs straight, they needed a break because it was hot. They quickly grabbed a table and sat down. Catching their breath, they ordered water from the waitress. The waitress came back two minutes later with their water and left. Out the corner of their eyes, they saw two guys approaching the table. Neither were in the mood to talk to anybody, they just wanted to enjoy they night out, and plus, Lashay's attention was occupied on Xavier. She wasn't thinking about nobody else. It had just dawned on Lashay that she hadn't talked to Xavier in a few days.

She had been so wrapped up with everything else she didn't have time to talk to him. Just as she pulled out her phone to text him, Xavier walked up.

"What's up ma?" Xavier said.

"Hey Baby, I was just about to text you." Lashay said getting up to hug him.

"Oh really? I haven't heard from you, where you been?" Xavier asked.

"It's been a lot going on, I'll tell you later." Lashay said.

"Alright, ma, we will talk." Xavier said.

"Hey, how y'all doing?" Chandelor said, coming from behind Xavier.

"Hey Chandelor, I didn't even see you." Lashay said.

"Hey cutie, I'm good." Lexi said on the sly hoping he didn't hear her.

Chandelor heard her but said nothing. He just winked at her, smiling, showing off his pearly whites. Lashay and Xavier picked up on it and smiled.

"Have my man been treating you good?" Chandelor asked Lashay.

"Yes, and I wouldn't have it any other way." Lashay told him.

"If he give you any problems, let me know." Chandelor said.

"Don't worry, I will." Lashay told him with a wink.

"Aye man, don't be trying to get on with my girl." Xavier said jokingly.

"She don't want me, man, and plus, I got my eye on someone already. " Chandelor said looking over at Lexi.

"You ain't ready." Lexi told him in flirty tone.

"I stay ready. The question is can you handle it?" Chandelor challenged.

"We going to let y'all talk for a minute. We going to the bar." Lashay said, as she stood up pulling Xavier's arm with her.

"Alright, y'all know what we want." Lexi and Chandelor said in unison.

The two just nodded their head, letting them know they had heard them as they walked off. Chandelor and Lexi began talking.

Chandelor thought Lexi was cute and wanted to holler at her, so this he was his chance, and he was going to take this opportunity.

Meanwhile, Lashay and Xavier were ordering drinks. As they waited, they made small talk. Xavier couldn't get enough of her in that dress. As soon as they left, he was going to beat the breaks off that tonight. Her curves in that dress were dangerous, and she was definitely turning heads. He just hoped for her sake, he didn't have to fuck nobody up over his.

"You gone get it when we get home for having this little ass dress on." Xavier whispered in her ear as he positioned her ass up against him so she could feel him.

"You always starting something." Lashay said giggled.

"It's your fault." Xavier said rubbing her ass.

"Really, it is?" Lashay asked, gently caressing him and licking his fingers.

"Stop playing, ma." Xavier said squirming and pulling back from her.

"You ready to go?" Lashay asked him, knowing he was.

Xavier kissed her lips instead of answering her and pulled her towards the exit. She knew what time it was. They were in their own world as they left. They forgot all about their friends and the drinks. Lashay had texted Lexi on their way out to let her know what was leaving, so she wouldn't worry. Xavier couldn't control his self, if he could, he would've had his way right then and there with Lashay.

She rode him like a cowgirl all the way into the waves of ecstasy. He didn't know how they had made it home with all the foreplay they were doing.

Finally, they made it inside of the house as they hungrily ripped each other's clothes off, never making it into the bedroom as they went at it in the kitchen. This wasn't love making this time, it was straight fucking. Moans and screams, skin slapping, toes curling, so many different positions were done, you would have to be a fly on the wall to see what really happened. They went at it steadily until they were exhausted. Both of them were so tired, they curled up on the couch with a blanket and went to sleep.

Lexi and Chandelor were still at Nikki's, dancing and talking it up. It was so apparent that they were into each other. One would assume they were a couple out having a good time and hadn't just met each other. They talked about everything from kids, past relationships, to future career goals. Intrigued by each other and not wanting to end the night or conversation so short, they decided to go to Denny's. Surprisingly, the diner wasn't packed at all, and they were seated right away. Continuing the conversation, it flowed as they placed their orders and throughout the meal. Neither had laughed or smiled so much in a while. It had been a nice outing in a while for both of them. Time flew by. It was six A.M. Chandelor followed Lexi home to make sure she got there safely. The two made plans to hang out later that day.

The next morning Xavier woke Lashay up early in the morning out of her sleep. He had a huge surprise for her and couldn't wait to see her reaction. It was five thirty in the morning, and their flight was leaving at seven thirty A.M. They didn't have much time to start getting ready. They still had to drive to the airport in Romulus.

"Baby, wake up." Xavier said shaking her.

"No, I'm sleepy. Give me a little while longer." Lashay said, rolling over away from him.

"You have to get up, or we're going to miss our flight." Xavier said smiling, knowing that would get her attention.

"What flight? We didn't plan a trip. Boy, stop messing with me." Lashay said with an attitude.

"You can go back to sleep on the plane." Xavier said rubbing her back.

"Xavier, if this is a way to get me up with you cause your up and can't sleep, it's not working today." Lashay said, trying to get comfortable again.

When she had a little bit of sleep, she could be very cranky.

"Fine, no Bahamas for you mean ass." Xavier said.

"Babe, are we really going, or you playing?" Lashay asked as she jumped out the bed fully awake.

"Ma, I wouldn't play with you about a trip. You should know how I am by now." Xavier said.

"Aww thanks, I always wanted to go." Lashay said.

"It's nothing, we can go wherever you want to go." Xavier said.

"Next time I want to go to Paris, since we can go wherever I want to go." Lashay said just to see what he was going to say.

"Stick with me, I'll show you the world and so much more." Xavier said, meaning every word.

She had him open.

"As long as you don't give me a reason to stray, you don't have to worry about me going away." Lashay said.

"I'm holding your word on that." Xavier told her.

"Okay, you can believe what I tell you or not, but my actions will tell you everything." Lashay said.

Xavier said nothing, he just took it all in. Only time would tell if what she said was true. She hadn't given him a reason to doubt her, and he wouldn't until shown otherwise.

"Get up and go get in the shower, we got to go." Xavier said.

"I'm about to get in now." Lashay said already having half her body through the bathroom door.

Xavier was right on her tail. Lashay got used to him getting in the shower with her. They got in, washed their bodies and was out with all in the span of twenty minutes. Quickly getting dressed and stuffing last minute items in their suitcases, they were all good to go. Xavier had packed the bags the night before so they were set. Getting to the airport on time would be the challenge.

Thirty minutes later, they arrived at the airport just in the nick of time. The attendant just had called the flight name and number, and people were already boarding the plane. A lady who worked there was nice enough to check them in the fast check line. Lashay ran into the gift shop to get nausea medicine, so she wouldn't get sick. She had a sensitive stomach. They were so relived they didn't miss their plane. At last, they made it to their seats in first class. Xavier paid extra just for the luxury. Lashay sat in awe, she never rode first class. She was going to play it cool and not embarrass herself.

Sixteen hours later, they arrived to the Bahamas. It was a straight shot there, no delays. Lashay and Xavier felt refreshed after their much needed nap on the plane. It was 100 degree weather, and the sun was beaming down on their bodies.

They couldn't wait to be in the air conditioning. A shuttle bus took them to their hotel. They checked in at The Paradise Atlantis Resort, it was a beautiful site. It had high ceilings, beautiful art on the walls, very neat and clean, indoor and outdoor pool, a big Jacuzzi, complimentary breakfast, and everything else you could dream of. The atmosphere was nice, and the people and hospitality were very friendly.

All week long they did something different. They visited the hotel's underground aquarium. They went to the Casino as well, winning a few stacks a piece. They would take boats and cabs to the hottest clubs and parties on the island. They tried all sorts of food and drinks. Even the people taught them some of their culture's dances. It really gave them a chance to spend uninterrupted time with one another including many candle light romantic dinners.

One day in particular, they went shopping. Xavier went into the jewelry store that they had and got Lashay a beautiful heart shaped pendant, earring set, with a 2.5 carat solitaire promise ring. He wanted to show her she meant something to him.

Lashay didn't know what to say when he gave it to her. In that moment, she knew this was real. That was all the conformation they needed.

On the plane on their way back to Detroit, Xavier grabbed Lashay's hand and turned her head until it was facing him.

"I love you, ma." Xavier said staring in her eyes lovingly.

"I... I.. I love you too, Xavier." Lashay replied back stuttering.

"Why you nervous, ma? I ain't propose yet." Xavier said, causing her to laugh.

"Shut up! It's been a minute since I felt like this about someone. This caught me off guard." Lashay said pouring it out there.

"Aww, my baby getting all mushy on me." Xavier said in a funny voice, finding it cute.

"Here you go, why you playin? You know love this." Lashay said pointing to herself as she smiled confidently.

"Yeah I do, now what?" Xavier asked "On some one hunned shit, I'm ready to make this official and be with you." Xavier said.

"We can make that happen. Two things though, don't fuck me over and don't lie to me." Lashay said not playing.

"I got you, boo." Xavier said, kissing her on the cheek.

"You better, three strikes and you're out." Lashay said, adding that in on the sly.

"The same rules apply to you too, Ms. Demanding." Xavier said, letting her know she wasn't off the hook either.

He knew women could be very sneaky at times.

"Wait until we get home, and I'll show you." Lashay said naughtily.

"You're a freak." Xavier said ready.

"I wonder where I got it from." Lashay fired back.

"Girl, you keep playing, and I'm going to have you on top of me right here." Xavier said dead serious.

"Don't tempt me, I ain't never scared." Lashay said challenging him.

"That's what your mouth say now." Xavier said knowing she would get scared and back down.

"Ok, put your money where your mouth is." Lashay said sliding her panties off discreetly underneath her skirt.

"You ain't said nothing but a word." Xavier briefly said as he tonged her down. For the next twenty five minutes, they got it in on the plane. Xavier had to cover Lashay's mouth as she screamed out loud sliding up and down on him. She rode him in the cowgirl position slowly. To other passengers it looked like she was sitting on his lap interacting with him. Heavy breathing and sighing could be heard as they tried to be quiet as possible as they both had an orgasm. Once they were done, they fixed their clothes quickly.

Lashay

Lashay was on the phone with her aunt.

"I think I'm in love and lust. Xavier has me on cloud nine, and I'm not coming down anytime soon. I really enjoyed our vacation. He is really going out of his way to do things for me. The gesture alone makes me smile. It's about time I found a winner. Since we made things official, it's no turning back now."

"No baby, it's not. You be careful, and you treat him right as well." Aunt Nicole said.

"Thanks, I will." Lashay said.

"You better, or we are going to have it out. I like Xavier for you." Aunt Nicole said.

"Oh Lord, he done won my family over." Lashay said laughing.

She was happy that they liked him. A week before the trip, Lashay took Xavier to meet her family. The women instantly fell in love with his charm. The men grilled him with questions about his expectations with Lashay. He was given a stern warning to treat Lashay right, or it would be his ass. Everything went smooth, and now Xavier was invited on her family outings.

"Girl hush!" Aunt Nicole said.

She was happy her niece had met someone who made her happy.

"I'll talk to you later." Lashay said hanging up the phone.

Lashay ate her dinner with a smile gracing her face. This relationship was the start of a new beginning.

Chapter 9: Trouble In Paradise

After a fun filled week in the Bahamas, the couple arrived back in Michigan. They both had things to take off, so they went their separate ways. But before they parted, they agreed on meeting later for dinner. Lashay went home to check her mail box. Looking through her mail, she couldn't believe her eyes as she read.

Hey Bae,

How you been doing? I been wondering what's been good with you. I know you tired of hearing this, but I'm a changed man. These past two years ain't been a joke. I ain't with that lame shit no more. I want to do something with my life. Shit, I ain't gone lie, I want you by my side, my ride or die. And I'm hoping you'll give me another chance. I heard from the board, and things are looking like they'll be going in my favor.

Love Montrell.

Lashay's palms began to sweat as she read the letter for the second time. This had to be a joke. How did he get my address? Who could have given it to him? I haven't talked to him in years. Now he wants to come back in my life just when I have moved on. I really don't need to be going there with him.

It took me too long to get over him, and I refuse to go through that again. I'm finally happy. He talking about he ain't about that life anymore, but I think it's just jail talk. Everybody gets saved and holy. I don't have the time or energy to go through that. Wait, while I'm thinking about all of this, how the fuck did he get my address? She pondered.

As the evening began, Lashay decided to call Lexi to tell her what happened, but she didn't answer. Then she called her cousin, Michelle, to see if she knew anything. Michelle reluctantly answered the phone. She was still salty from their last conversation.

"Hey, guess who I just got a letter from?" Lashay said.

"Who?" Michelle asked wanting to know.

"Montrell, girl, for the life of me I can't figure out how he got my address." Lashay said.

"Ooh girl, my baby daddy, Kevin, is in the same prison. So I asked Kev to give him your address." Michelle said.

"I really wish you would have consulted me first instead of giving my address out. It's a reason why he doesn't have it.

I haven't spoken to him in years, and I wasn't trying to rekindle the relationship at all." Lashay said.

"How was I supposed to know? It ain't like I talk to you." Michelle said.

"That's why you should have asked." Lashay said.

"Well, I didn't, so get over it." Michelle said sarcastically.

Lashay felt herself going there, so she just hung up on her.

She concealed the letter putting it in her drawer. There was no particular reason for her keeping it. Her mood instantly changed from good to being completely puzzled. Xavier called her phone, but she didn't answer. She honestly didn't know what to say to him and really didn't want to be bothered with anyone at this point.

Lashay felt a string of different unexplainable emotions that she didn't expect. Why was she reflecting on the past? This is too much.

"I would be dumb as hell to go back to him. And I don't have time for the drama." She said out loud as she rattled off. "Damn, I gotta figure this out." Her last words spoken as she pondered pacing the floor back in forth.

Beginning to get a headache, she decided to lie down.

All week she had been moping around and wondering what to do. Every time Xavier called, she wouldn't answer, her appetite was barely there and sleep didn't happen at all. It was starting to take a toll on her physically and emotionally. Her work performance was the only thing that wasn't affected by this. No matter what she did, what may have happened, and what was happening, she wouldn't allow anything or anyone to interfere with her work. One thing for sure she, was going to get this off her chest. Grabbing a pen and a piece of paper, she began to write a response back to Montrell.

Montrell,

Oh wow I can't believe you have the audacity to write me. What do you expect from me? You want me to tell you I miss you and want to be with you. Well you thought wrong. There will never be an "us" again. As far you having another chance with me, you can kill that dream. You must be crazy to think I'm going to hold you down. Do I look like boo boo the fool? I don't take care of grown men, and I will not be anybody's prison wife. The moment has passed. I have moved on and so should you.

Sincerely, Lashay.

After she was done completing the letter, she addressed it to him, put it in an envelope, and sealed it while laying it down on her nightstand. She didn't know whether she was going to mail it to him or not. Needing some advice, she called her mom and explained to her what happened.

"Hey ma." Lashay said to her mother soon as she answered and said Hello. "Guess who contacted me today." Lashay said.

"Who?" Gina asked.

"Montrell, do you remember him?" Lashay replied.

"Yeah Bigboi, oh Lord, what does he want?" Gina asked.

"Asking me for another chance." Lashay replied.

"You can be the fool if you want to again, that boy took you through it. Haven't you had enough? I raised you better than that. You don't listen just hardheaded." Gina said all in one breath.

She was getting fed up with this conversation.

"Momma, you don't have to remind me, I get it." Lashay said already feeling the annoyance coming in her system from her mother's words.

"So, if you know then it shouldn't keep crossing your mind. It shouldn't even be given a second thought." Gina said scolding her.

"I don't know what it is. I guess it's still some unresolved feelings there." Lashay said unsure of her feelings.

"Girl, wake up. If he didn't treat you right the first time, what makes you think that this time will be any different? Won't shit change. That's just jailbird talk, of course he's going to sweet talk you and tell you all the things you want to hear, so he can have somewhere to lay his head at and someone to take care of him. I know you would be dumb enough to do it." Gina said, keeping it real with her.

She had been through that in one of her past relationships in her younger days, so she knew exactly what her daughter was going through.

"Tell me how you really feel." Lashay said sarcastically.

"Well, somebody needs to tell you because you're acting crazy." Gina said shouting.

"I hear you, mama." Lashay said, hoping her mother got the hint to leave it alone she was going hard.

"You better." Gina said.

"Alright, let me get off this phone." Lashay said, rushing her off the phone.

"Just because you think your grown now don't mean you have to forget about us. Yo ass ain't never too old to get a whopping remember that." Gina said in a chastising tone.

"I'll be over there Saturday." Lashay said just so she could shut up.

"Don't be rushing me off the phone, because you mad and all in your feelings." Gina said going there.

"Mama, I'm cooking, I have to get the food out of the oven before it burns." Lashay said truthfully.

"What are you cooking?" Gina asked her.

"Baked chicken, lemon rice and green beans." Lashay answered.

"Where's my plate?" Gina asked, her stomach instantly began growling and her mouth watered like she could physically taste the delicious food.

Her daughter could throw down in the kitchen.

"Come get it." Lashay replied.

She wasn't about to bring it to her.

"Put me some up, I'll come get it tomorrow."
Gina said setting a reminder on her phone of it.

"Okay I will, bye." Lashay said, grabbing one of
the plastic containers filling it up with food for her
momma.

"Bye, I love you." Gina said, hanging up the
phone.

Lashay got off the phone, took her food out of the
oven, fixed her plate and then ate. Along with dinner, she
had a glass of Sweet Red Wine by Shutter Home. She
needed a therapy session, and she knew just the person to
call, Lexi.

Lexi had been really busy these days with
Chandelor. They were so cute together. She had finally
moved out of the Martin Luther King apartments. She
had found a three bedroom house in Warren. The girls
were going to love it. She had even enrolled in school for
nursing in the spring. Things were definitely looking up
for her. She was finally getting herself together, so she
could build a better future for her and her children.

Lashay called Lexi and told her to meet her at Flood's downtown. It was a lounge with a mature, mixed crowd. They had great music, good food and the atmosphere was enjoyable. They pulled up at the same time. They greeted each other with a hug as they walked in the entrance. The music was jumping as they played in the background an oldie but goodie song, "Happy" by Pharrel. People were dancing, talking and having a good time. Stopping directly at the bar, they both ordered Long Islands. They told the bartender to make them strong. Immediately they sat down, and Lexi began talking.

"Girl, why Monty been trying to talk to me?" Lexi said with an attitude.

"What?" Lashay asked in disbelief.

"Yes girl, the other day he gone tell me I'm looking good and asked me could he take me out to dinner." Lexi said rolling her neck.

"For real?" Lashay asked puzzled.

"I laughed at him and told him to gone somewhere." Lexi said.

"What is wrong with these guys? They be on some other shit."

"Don't I know it?" Lexi said. "Ain't nobody got time for that."

"I'm going to kick your ass for pushing my brother to the curb." Lexi said, calling Xavier by his nickname she had given him and getting straight to the point with her.

"Bye Felicia, you ain't gone do nothing." Lashay said, flipping her off.

"Don't let this cute face fool you." Lexi said, cheesing with a big grin.

"Whatever."

Lashay just laughed knowing nothing wouldn't happen between them.

"You heard me, heifer." Lexi said playing around with her.

"I just don't know what to say." Lexi said confused.

"Well you better say something, or you're going to lose him."

"I'm going to talk to him." Lashay said, knowing she really needed to.

"You better, or I'm going to do it." Lexi said, serious as a heart attack.

"Okay, now stop getting on my nerves." Lashay said, just to get a reaction out of her.

She knew Lexi was serious and would make good on her word. Before Lexi could reply, she changed the subject.

"Let me show you this letter Montrell sent me." She said to her pulling it out her Michael Kors' purse.

Lexi snatched the letter out of her hand and read it. Her eyes widened big as saucers with every word that was read. As soon as she was getting ready to tell her what she thought, Millian walked in. Lashay wasn't paying any attention as she ordered another drink. She turned around just as he walked up to them.

"What is she doing here?" Lashay said asking Lexi.

"I told her she could come. I didn't think it would be a big deal."

"You really get on my last nerves with this always inviting her when it's just supposed to be us. You know I don't like her at all." Lashay said not hiding the fact that she didn't like her.

"Don't start, Shay, damn." Lexi said, not feeling her attitude.

"You could of warned me." Lashay said snotty.

"I didn't, so get over it." Lexi said done with the conversation.

Clearing her throat, making her presence be known, Millian spoke.

"Hey y'all," Million said in a fake voice.

They both said hey back, but Lashay's 'hey' was so dry and rude.

"What are yall talking about?" Millian asked peaking over Lashay's shoulder as she looked at the text Xavier sent her.

Millian discreetly took out her phone, storing Xavier's number that she remembered.

"None of your fucking business," Lashay replied, venom all in her voice.

"It looks like it's everybody business the way this letter is spread on the table for the world to see."

"Let's see what it says." Millian said grabbing the letter up so fast before anyone had a chance to react.

"Give me my shit back, you bitch." Lashay said not caring she had crossed the line.

"Whoa, chill out." Lexi said.

"Who you calling a bitch? Bitch!" Millian said.

"I'm talking to you, I didn't stutter. You can try me tonight if you want to." Lashay said ready to fight.

"You know what? Your crippled ass ain't even worth it." Millian said walking away.

"She's a stupid hoe. I don't know how you deal with her." Lashay said ordering a shot of tequila.

"Y'all are giving me too much in one night." Lexi said.

She couldn't believe they were acting like that. That was so high school.

"I'm leaving." Lashay said getting up.

"Are you sure you can drive?" Lexi said, making sure her friend was okay to get home safe.

"I'm fine. I'll call you when I get home." Lashay said.

She was a little buzzed, nothing major, or Lexi wouldn't have her driving. She paid her tab and gave her a hug goodbye promising to get with her again soon.

On her way home, Lashay had one person on her mind as she drove to the destination. Lashay paced outside his place. Here goes nothing, she thought to herself, as she knocked on the door. No more than ten seconds had passed when Xavier answered.

They looked into each other's eyes dazed.

"We need to talk," Lashay said.

Xavier hesitantly let her in. Millian had just called privately him and told him everything. He didn't even know how she got his number. Of course, she put her own twist on things. Then she sent him a screen shot of the letter. Xavier became irate as he read each word. He couldn't even think straight. Throwing his phone across the wall only infuriated him more when the screen fractured. Xavier wanted to fuck her up.

"I know about the letter." Xavier said intensely, as his veins throbbed in the side of his neck.

"Baby, I can explain." Lashay said shaken.

That fucking bitch, she thought to herself. I got something for that ass. Before she could get her words out, Xavier chimed in.

He began laughing hysterically and turned to Lashay and said, "Do you know how many people told me I could do better? Do you know how many times individuals have asked me why I was so committed to someone such as yourself?" He chuckled. "Since we have been together so many women came on to me, with offers that were hard to turn down, I might add.

I could be with someone much more competent than you. I have been tailoring my life for your incapable ass. I could be with someone on my level, living life." Pausing in the middle of his rant he said, "Oh shit, I'm so rude, ah would you like a chair. Your legs must be killing you!" Xavier said sarcastically, with a look that could cut though stone. When she didn't answer, he continued on. "Do you know why all those men you were with, in the past, fucked you and left? Well, I have the answer for you. No one wants to deal with your limitations, but it is nothing to lay you on your back and get things done. I mean it's not like it takes any hard work on your part!"

Piecing her words together, trying to stop the crack in her voice as she spoke.

"Tell me this, if I'm such a problem in your life, why are you still wasting your time? Why do you come back for more? You stay in bed in between my legs. That's not what you were saying when we was fucking. I don't get no complaints. You must not know about me. I'll have another you in a minute. You are not irreplaceable, hunny. I know somebody who likes it. Would you like for me to call him?" She pulled out her phone to hand it to him.

"Obviously it's something you like. I thought you were different. Clearly I was wrong. You ain't shit!"

Even after she said what she said, she just wanted him to feel the same hurt that she did. Lashay knew he had been drinking, however, it didn't take the sting out of his words. She stood there frozen in pain. She had no words. She was in dismay. She couldn't stop the tears from rolling down her face as she walked away. Unbeknownst to them, there was someone watching them.

Lashay

Lashay sat there pondering as she browsed online. I'm so confused. I don't know what to do. Xavier just let me have it and probably don't want to be with me. Montrell fucked up my head with that letter. I can't go back to being stupid now. My emotions are all over the place. I don't need anything else crazy to happen. What am I going to do? Retail therapy always made her feel better, so she did some shopping to distract her mind.

Xavier

Xavier was playing a game of pool at a sports bar. A woman walked up to him trying to get his number. He turned her down. He couldn't stop thinking about her. Lashay is on some straight up and down bullshit. She won't see me, or answer my calls. I mean, damn, she must be cheating, or another nigga must be occupying her time. I'm not about to keep waiting around for her to make up her mind. If she don't get it together, I'm going to start doing me. I love her, but what does love have to do with it? I hope we can work it out, but for now, I'm gone back the fuck off. Maybe she'll come to her senses. I'd be wrong as hell if I cheated, or I pulled that bullshit. Xavier just chilled with a few of his boys for the night.

Chapter 10: Torn

Lashay was so hurt by Xavier's words, she couldn't think straight. She sat in the dark, listening to Mary J. Blige, "Not Gone Cry" on repeat. Mary's words were soothing to her soul. It was like the song was made just for her as she was singing along. She looked in the mirror feeling disgusted by her image. Her self-esteem hit an all-time low, and she thought no one would ever want her again. Her hair was all over her head matted, and she was still in her clothes from the night before. All she did was cry her eyes out, her body wouldn't allow her to do anything else. She sat there in pity as she started to doubt and question herself. "Is it some truth to what he's saying?" "Is that the reason why they really left?" "Am I not good enough?" "Did they really see me as just a jump off?" Those were the things flowing through her mind as she destroyed her room.

"Fuck him. I don't need him." Lashay said as she threw her lamp into the wall not affected by the piercing sounds as it broke in pieces.

His words echoed in her head as she proceeded to the bathroom. She gathered his things from the closet and sat them in the bathtub.

Quickly she went into the kitchen and grabbed the lighter fluid and a pack of matches then ran back into the bathroom and set it into a flaming blaze. As the fire began to grow, she stood there and admired the flames not realizing the intensity of it until the smoke filled her lungs and the smoke detector began to go off and beep loudly. Smoke was everywhere, and black fire marks got on the walls. That's when she noticed her bathtub was burning up. Coming to her senses, she snapped out of it.

"Oh shit! What the hell did I just do?" She yelled.

Panicking, she went and got her fire extinguisher, instantly putting the fire out. It was a wrap, her bathroom needed to be repaired immediately. She made a mental note to call a repair person in the morning.

She was glad she had an extra bathroom downstairs. She would have to use that one for now. She went downstairs to the other bathroom to take a long shower. Throwing a dress on, she felt a little better. Calming down, she sat on the couch catching her breath, drinking a glass of water. I need to call off work. I can't do it today. Lashay called her boss and asked for two weeks of her vacation time off. They approved it. She was going to use this time to relax and get her mind right.

A few days after, on a Tuesday to be exact, she was sitting on the edge of the bed sobbing staring at Xavier's picture. Suddenly, the doorbell rang. She jumped up out of her trance and quickly wiped her face. She went into the bathroom, stared at the mirror and told herself, she was okay. Walking slowly to the door, she tripped over the rug.

"I am really tripping." She said as she reached the door.

She looked out of the peephole and when she seen what she thought she seen, she thought she could have fainted. Instantly she got this burst of energy. She closed her eyes and opened them. To her surprise, it was Montrell, who she once was deeply in love with. To his surprise, he was greeted with a hard blow to his face. She was viciously hitting him while saying every cuss word in the book to him.

He tried to block her and said, "Whoa, whoa. What are you doing? I thought you would be happy to see me."

She was still hollering as she hit him. Forcing him to grab and pick her up so she could stop. That only infuriated her more as she punched him in the mouth busting his lip. He struggled to get her in the house. Once he got her sitting her down on the couch he spoke.

"Damn girl, have you been working out? You busted my lip." Montrell said, touching his bloody, leaking mouth. He grabbed the napkin he had in pocket from earlier to stop the bleeding. "What the hell is wrong with you?"

She sat there silent looking at him. While sitting there watching her breath, he continued on.

"It's me, Mon, don't you miss me? What's going on with you?"

She couldn't take it anymore. She burst out in tears realizing what was going on. Montrell grabbed her, she couldn't keep the fight up. Allowing him to console her, he rubbed her back and ran his fingers through her hair.

"It's going to be alright, ma. I am here for you." He said kissing her on the cheek caressing her hand.

All of sudden she pushed him off her.

"Are you ready to talk about it?"

Instead of responding, she just stared at him with this seductive look in her eyes. She started to aggressively but passionately kiss him on his neck. She climbed on top of him unbuckling his jeans pushing her panties to the side as she inserted him deeply inside. She let out a sigh. Ten hard deep strokes later, he was moaning and pulling her hair as he drilled away. Getting into it, she started moving her hips in circles bouncing up and down, meeting him thrust for thrust. No words were spoken, all you could her were their moans and their skin slapping together. Sweat and cum filled their bodies as they had passionate sex all night.

Laying in the bed quiet thinking, "What the hell did I just do," she hopped up, gathered his clothes and made him leave.

"You gotta go."

Not even giving him a chance to say anything, she slammed the door in his face. Although she was upset with what she had just done, she was stunned by his immaculate performance. He caressed her in all the right ways. His hardness made her climax multiple times, and she couldn't get over how he had made her feel. Montrell had never put it down and pleased her as he just did.

It amazed her how quickly she was able to climax when that's something he wasn't able to do for her. She laid there thinking, eventually feeling confused saying to herself, "Did I make a mistake?" "Is this meant to be?" "Has he really changed?" The questions invaded her thoughts as she went to sleep.

She woke up to a text message that read, 'Hey beautiful, I really enjoyed you last night and I just can't stop thinking about it. Felt like old times. I'm sure you didn't want that to happen cause you kicked my ass out like I was a nigga on the street. Lol but on the real, I'm really concerned about you and I want to talk about it. Can I please come over? So we can talk. Let me know holla at me.'

She read the text over and over again then decided to respond. 'Yes you can come over!!' He came over fast as if he was waiting at the corner. Damn he didn't waste no time, she thought to herself as she looked out the peephole. Opening the door, he ducked putting his hands in front of his face.

Laughing she said, "Umm what are you doing?"

He replied, "I'm protecting myself. Last time I was greeted with a blow to the face." Shrugging him off, laughing again she said, "You so stupid, come in."

She stepped to the side so he could enter. Lashay expressed to him why she treated him the way she did. It was all the ill feelings she was harboring towards him for breaking her heart. Montrell sincerely apologized to her. His intentions were never to hurt her. He loved her deeply. He was just too caught up in the street life to realize what he had in her. Montrell tried to make a move by kissing her on the lips. Immediately she stopped him, pushing him back.

"Stop, I'm not ready for this."

He said, "I thought you wanted to continue from yesterday."

"No, yesterday I was vulnerable. I didn't mean to lead you on."

He respected her wishes and let her be. They chilled for the remainder of the day chopping it up and reminiscing on old times. Montrell went home late with thoughts of making things right with Lashay.

The next day he came over and took Lashay to Red Lobster for lunch. From that day on, the two were inseparable. They began spending more and more time together. He wined and dined her and showered her with gifts. Old feelings she thought were gone came resurfacing backing clouding and confusing her feelings for him even more. It was like a tug of war pulling on her heart between who was right for her, and what she knew was no good for her. What was she to do?

Montrell surprised Lashay one night with a romantic candle light dinner. The ambiance was nice and mellow, smooth jazz played on the Bose stereo system. Both were dressed up for the occasion. Montrell had a nice white short-sleeve button up shirt with a tan pair of cargo pants with some brown dress shoes. Lashay had on strapless short black dress with wedges. Tonight he was on a mission, and he wasn't stopping until it was complete. He hired a private chef to cook them a dinner that consisted of tilapia, red potatoes, green beans, and a house salad with fresh Hawaiian rolls with a glass of red wine. For dessert was homemade Lemon pound cake from scratch.

They were so stuffed, they could hardly move. Small talk from the day's events and laughter from the two filled the room. Leaving the table, the two decided to go watch a movie in Lashay's bedroom. She picked out the new DVD, "About Last Night" from her movie collection. She popped in the movie and sat down on her bed propped up against the pillows. He did the same sitting next to her, trying to cuddle with her, but she rejected it. She just wasn't feeling it or him right now, and she didn't know why. Instead, she just grabbed his hand and held it. It wasn't what he wanted, but he was content and wasn't going to pressure her. Throughout the movie they laughed until their stomachs hurt. Towards the end of the movie, she began to get sleepy and rolled over on her side and drifted off to sleep.

Snuggling up next to her, he gave her a kiss and tried his hardest to fall asleep. An hour had passed, and he felt restless. Tired of tossing and turning, he gave up. He began kissing Lashay on her shoulder then her neck, hoping to get her attention. Stirring a little in her sleep, she paid him no mind as she turned over. Caressing her thigh softly, Lashay moaned loudly still asleep. Montrell took this as an opportunity to keep going.

Traveling further up, he reached her panties, ripping them off. He couldn't control his self any longer, he had to taste her. Slowly licking her sweet pearl up and down it heightened his arousal making him want more. Lashay awoke to his tongue deep inside her.

"Oh shit!" Was her only words spoken as she fucked his face.

Sticking two fingers inside while he continued to please her made her buck and thrust her hips towards him.

"Yes, keep going," Lashay said to him getting wetter.

"Umm, you taste good." Montrell replied, rubbing her nipples as her body was in sync with his every move.

Fifteen minutes later, she had a mind blowing orgasm that made her whole body shake. He didn't stop until he sucked her dry. Her juices dripped off his chin as he switched positions to enter her.

"Can I have it, ma?" he asked.

Lashay didn't say another word, nodding her head yes and opening her legs. He just wanted a quickie, he didn't want to make love, going in with a hard thrust.

"Slow down, I'm not going anywhere." Lashay said as he quickly pumped, beating her walls up.

"Shit." He said, trying not to cum, so he kissed her to keep himself distracted.

Lashay moaned in pleasure as she thought of Xavier.

"Get it together." She said to herself kissing him back like she was enjoying it.

That excited him as he went deeper. Getting tired, he stopped and laid on his side. He lifted Lashay's leg in the air and plunging inside, not missing a beat. Lashay was really into it now as she fantasized about Xavier stroking her, throwing it back at him.

"You like that?"

"Yes baby, keep going. I'm almost there." Lashay said.

"Is that right?" Montrell asked going even faster.

"Yes, Xavier, make me cum baby." Lashay said in pleasure not realizing what she just did.

Montrell heard it but pretended that he didn't.

"Cum with me." He said.

Right on que, Lashay's cum was running down both their legs and all over him.

"Xavier, I love you" Lashay said as she finished.

"Bitch, what the fuck did you say?" Montrell said, heatedly stopping in the middle of his stroke, mad he was just about to cum as well.

"What?" Lashay asked playing dumb.

She knew she had fucked up.

"I will fucking hurt you, my name ain't Xavier." Montrell said choking her neck with both of his fat hands, cutting off her air supply.

Lashay struggled to get him off her, clawing at him with her nails into his skin drawing blood.

"I can't breathe, get off me." Lashay said above a whisper punching him on his back.

"You wrong as hell, man." Montrell said releasing her, breathing hard sounding like a bear.

"You got me fucked up to think I'm just going to sit here and let you put your hands on me. You crazy as hell." Lashay said ready to shoot.

She got up and went to the night stand drawer pulling out her Taser. Knowing she was wrong for calling him Xavier's name, she'd be the first one to admit that was a big mistake on her part, but he did not have to put his hands on her.

Only cowards and women beaters did that, in her opinion. Shoot first, ask questions later, was her motto, but in this case, things were a little different. She had to handle this delicately tonight. She wasn't spending the night in nobody's jail. He had his back turned towards the wall as she snuck up behind him and tazed him with no remorse. Montrell never had a chance to react as his body shook. It was just enough to put him in shock. Lashay stood there laughing at him.

"You crazy." Montrell said getting up, the sting was wearing off.

"We'll see who's crazy when I call your probation officer. I bet you'll think twice next time." Lashay said.

"I just got out, and now you want to send a nigga back!" Montrell yelled.

"Sounds like a personal problem to me, goodbye." Lashay said, waving him off.

"This isn't over, bitch." He said walking towards the door.

"I'm the bitch you're going to miss, don't text or call me. We done." Lashay said with a smile that left him flabbergasted.

"You don't mean that." Montrell said knowing differently.

"I can show you better than I can tell you. I asked you to leave. Why are you still standing here?" Lashay said with her hands on hip rocking her leg with nothing but her t-shirt on.

Lashay was beyond pissed and was ready for him to vanish.

"You on some bull shit, I'm out. You think your lonely now, wait until tonight, you'll be begging me to come back."

Montrell walked out without another word, slamming the door so hard she thought he broke it off the hinges.

"Fuck my life." Lashay said going back her bedroom.

It was time for her to reevaluate some things. At least she would have a piece of mind.

Montrell

As a stress reliever, Montrell decided to go play some ball. Did this bitch call me another nigga name then have the audacity to kick me out her house?

I can't believe this shit. What a fucking way to come home. I gotta find out who the fuck this Xavier nigga is. Lashay must have thought I was playing when I told her she would always be mine. She got another thing coming if she thinks I'm just going to sit back and watch her be with the next nigga. The thoughts triggered his mind as he played a one on one game.

Lashay

Lashay began to clean up the mess they made. As she began to vacuum the carpet her thoughts came back to her.

"Montrell has lost his mind. I bet he'll think twice before he ever puts his hands on me. I know I fucked up big time calling him Xavier name. I really missed my boo. I want him back. Montrell can't be the man I need him to be. Why did he have to come back now? Why did I have sex with him? Everything was going good until he came back with his shenanigans. I done created a monster. I know he ain't gone let it go. I got to clean up the mess I made. I just hope it ain't too late.

How do I make it right? Where do I start? Will he forgive me? I can only imagine what's going through Xavier's head. This is Jerry Springer type shit." She said to herself out loud as she looked out her bedroom window.

For the most part, Xavier has been drinking himself in a frenzy for the past week and barely eating. Even that was by force. As he was sitting there sipping on his third glass of Hennessey trying to cope with the aftermath of what happened between him and Lashay, R. Kelly's TP2 CD was on, but Xavier had "I Don't Mean It" on replay. He was in a funk and couldn't shake it off. It was like she had some type of hold on him.

Xavier realized what he did was fucked up and wished he could take it all back. He didn't mean what he had said, he was just so mad at her. No matter how hard he tried to front like he didn't miss her, he did, or wasn't thinking about her, he was. Xavier loved her. There weren't any other words to describe how he felt or his actions towards her. If he didn't, he wouldn't have responded to her the way that he did. A real man would only be able to admit it to himself.

He never meant to break her down and make her cry. He wanted to be the reason she smiled. Xavier didn't want her to say goodbye to him and what they had. He just wanted to hear her voice and make things right, but every time he picked up the phone to call, he couldn't. One way or another, he was going to get his girl back. She fumbled his heart. Lashay was his high, and he was in need of his next hit. Finally he dialed Lashay's number, but all he got was her voicemail.

"Damn, I'm acting like a female with all this mushy shit, this right here ain't cool." Xavier said frustrated, cutting the music off.

Powering the Television on to the BET Awards, Chris Brown was performing, getting the crowd hyped. Xavier sang along word for word feeling the music.

Out of nowhere, there was a knock on the door. Xavier wondered who it could be. He wasn't expecting company. Checking his appearance in the mirror that sat on the wall, he decided looked decent. He had on a grey wife beater with dark blue basketball shorts and Nike Men's flip flops. His facial hair was scruffy, and he needed a hair-cut badly. Two and a half weeks ago was the last time he had one, and he didn't care.

Whoever it was, they would have to excuse him this time. Opening the door to see who it was, he instantly frowned and gave her a look that could kill.

The infamous Millian stood there wearing a nude, sheer, see-through dress that left nothing to the imagination, pairing it with matching heels.

"How the hell do you know where I live?" Xavier said looking at her side ways.

"It's for me to know and for you to find out." Millian said in a childish manner.

Xavier knew right then and there that she didn't have all of her screws.

"What do you want?" Xavier asked straight to the point.

"I want you, are you gone let me in or nah?" Millian said popping her gum and twirling her hair, lifting up her dress so he could see she didn't have anything else on.

"Nawl, I'm good. It aint even that type of party." Xavier said trying to let her down gently, so he wouldn't hurt her feelings.

"I guess I have to be physically challenged to get some attention from you huh?" Millian said insultingly, desperately mimicking Lashay's walk looking stupid.

"You ignorant as hell. First off, I was never nor will I ever be interested in you.
You're a grimy, sneaky, trifling hoe that is so desperate for a man that she'll stoop to the lowest level of them all and try to fuck her friend's man. That's sad, you really need some help." Xavier said on fire.

She was dirty and foul. He wasn't about to let her just keep talking about Lashay that way whether they were together or not. He closed the door in her face. Before it could fully close, Millian caught it with her hand.

"Wait, I have something you might be interested in seeing." Millian said excitedly.

"How many times do I have to tell your slow ass no?" Xavier asked her, wanting to beat the breaks off her.

Ignoring him, she showed him the picture of Lashay and Montrell kissing one night they went out on the date.

"Your precious Lashay aint so innocent after all." Millian said.

She had photo shopped the photo making it look like more than what it was.

"Go on somewhere with that shit." Xavier said.

He couldn't stand the sight of the woman he loved with her ex.

"I bet you didn't know about all the letters they been writing back and forth to each other this whole time." Millian said hoping he'd believe her.

"You'll say anything huh." Xavier said not buying it.

"Why would I lie about this? I thought you should know about her and her new man." Millian said, smirking and handing him a few of the fake letters she had handwritten.

"Come in while I read these for a minute." Xavier said letting her in; this peaked his interest.

"Thanks, its hot as hell. " Millian said walking over to the couch sitting down.

Summer was in effect, and the 89 degree weather felt like 100 degrees with a little breeze. The night's temperature was finally dropping, making it a little cooler.

Millian barely could contain herself as images of her and Xavier having sex filled her head. In her mind, Xavier was just playing hard to get, but once she made her move, he would cave in.

"Do you mind if I have a drink?" Millian said batting her lashes with a closed smile fanning herself with hands.

"Knock yourself out, the bar is over there." Xavier said pointing his finger in the direction of the sports bar he had built when he first moved in that sat in the corner of the living room.

"So tell me, hun, do you ever get bored with her? I mean from the looks of it there isn't much she can do." Millian said, being sarcastic.

Xavier sat ignoring her sarcasm while he continued to read. Millian tried and tried to gain his attention, but it seemed as though nothing was working, so she sat quietly and sipped her extra strong drink.

The more Xavier read, the more things did not make sense. He realized that the writing in the letter looked similar to a letter she had written him when she first attempted to hook up with him.

He then threw the letters across the table acting upset smacking his lips and mumbled under his breath.

"What was that, boo?" Milliam replied.

"I can't stand a lying ass bitch, I really just got played. Damn!" He then looked at Millian and said, "So let me ask you this, why are you so interested in tearing down the next woman, who happens to be doing something productive and bettering herself, I mean really what's it to you?"

Millian looked puzzled, tongue tied and could not respond right away.

Millian was quiet for a second and then quickly replied, "I'm not interested in her or what she is doing, I couldn't care less. Once my modeling career take off, which will be real soon, I'm gone be more than just the shit, niggas gone think I'm Tyra Banks." She laughed and added, "I mean, let's be real, why are you so interested in someone like her? Look at her, she will always need help. Hell, it looks like she's gonna fall every time she walks. You need someone to protect you, her ass can't even run let alone protect you. You seem so desperate. You used to enjoy bitches falling at your feet, now you the one that's falling, what the fuck, Xav.

But on the real, I can make you feel like she can't and never will, the thought of her being with you is fucking up my high, so why don't you just come over her and let me give you a sample of this good good," Millian replied devilishly.

Xavier looked at her in disgust because at this point he knew that she had written the letters and just wanted her to leave. He however, wanted to make her feel just as low and degraded as he knew he had made Lashay feel.

Xavier had always disliked when someone made fun of Lashay or even stared at her too long. He was so defensive that he would always threaten a person and make them apologize to her on the spot. Millian's nasty and hurtful words made Xavier re-live the moment that he regretted, and one that he wanted to forget, which was being disrespectful and saying similar hurtful words to Lashay.

Xavier knew he was wrong for what he had said to Lashay, and deep down, he felt so ashamed that he wanted to cry. Just the thought of it made Xavier even more frustrated and angry.

He walked slowly to Millian and said, "Girl, you a mess." He chuckled a bit and said, "So you really want this, huh?"

Millian replied, "Yes," with so much desperation.

Xavier then said to her, "Why don't you polish it off first?"

She looked into his eyes and said, "My pleasure baby, I promise you won't forget this."

He allowed her to pull his pants down while she was on her knees assuming the position. Just as she closed her eyes about to indulge in his thickness, he pissed all over her face.

She stood up and screamed, "What the fuck! Nigga, are you crazy? What the hell was that for?"

As she wiped her face looking disgusted, Xavier said calmly, "Like I told you before, I can't stand a lying ass bitch, now get the fuck out of my house."

She looked at him with a hurtful look, while trying to contain herself to keep from crying she stated, "Nigga, this ain't over, and don't worry, charges will not be pressed, but you gone get yours, you and that crippled bitch."

He laughed as he made sure she exited his home and told her, "You're the one that's desperate, with yo broke ratchet ass. Go suck a dick hoe." He yelled out, watching her tires screech as she sped away giving him the finger.

All he did was shake his head. That broad is off her rocker. He was going to have to watch himself around her, knowing she would pull another stunt. These hoes weren't loyal to themselves let alone anyone else. Ain't no telling what else she might do.

Xavier dragged himself up off the couch and headed to the shower and turned on the television he had installed and mounted on top in the center of the wall to Fox News. He needed to see what was going on in the world before he went to check on the club. He scrubbed his body until he felt clean. As he was hopping out the shower, he couldn't believe his eyes or ears as he stood in shock reading the caption. What is the world coming to?

"Two women are injured and are in critical condition and fighting for their lives at Harper Hospital. All within the hour, one woman is brutally raped and severally beaten. And the other collides with a semi-truck that ended up in an explosion on I-94 freeway. Both victims are getting rushed to the hospital as we speak. Victims aren't related to each other. Doctors speculate that they won't survive longer than 24 hours. More details coming at 11 pm stay tuned."

Just as Xavier began to walk away to get dressed, he heard his phone ringing on the end table in the living room. Rushing to answer the phone, he couldn't understand what the person was saying on the other end of the line from all of the crying they were doing.

"Who is this?" Xavier asked.

"It's Lexi, Xavier." Lexi said hysterical, barely controlling her sobbing.

"What's up? I just heard some fucked up shit on the news, man, about these two women." Xavier said thinking that what happened was such a tragedy.

"That's what I am calling you about. You have to get to the hospital now! Lashay was one of those women who got injured." Lexi barely got the words out hoping her friend lived.

"Oh shit! I'm on my way right now." Xavier said, yelling and scattering to put on anything as he hurried and grabbed his keys running to his Benz.

He could hardly think straight.

"Okay, I'll see you there." Lexi said hanging up already in the parking lot getting ready to go in.

"Alright man, just stay strong." Xavier said throwing the phone down in the cup holder speeding off running through every red light to get to his baby.

"Damn, she just has to pull through." Xavier said as choked up tears welled in his eyes, blurring his vision.

As he was flying on the freeway, he arrived to the hospital in twenty minutes flat. Xavier felt a cold chill go up his spine as he walked through the doors. He couldn't stand hospitals. The smell, the vibe, and the food was disgusting. It made his stomach turn. Somebody was always sick or dying.

Just as he was approaching the front desk, he heard this gut wrenching scream.

"Lashay nooooo noooo oh God please not my baby!" Gina screamed loudly, falling to her knees rocking back and forth curling up in a fetal position on the floor.

To be continued..........

ABOUT THE AUTHOR

Shanicia Jackson resides in Detroit Michigan where she currently has wrote and completed her First debut novel An imperfect love has no limits and many more to follow. She started off as an avid reader and a poet and eventually her hobby of just writing turned into a full fledge story. Her goal is to continue writing stories with a purpose that will inspire others. When she isn't writing Shanicia volunteers in her spare time. Her favorite hobbies are shopping, reading, and hanging out with family and friends. Her Moto is: HARD WORK DOES PAY OFF and NEVER GIVE UP ON YOUR DREAMS, MIRACLES HAPPEN EVERY DAY!